MW01613177

Her shoulders t
all before Dariu
response. She tucked her hand and its scar into one
of her coat pockets.

The scar that matched Darius's.

The scar that had changed his life.

The scar that would have been much worse had a little girl named Evelyn Myers not protected him with everything she had.

Now, scar out of sight, there might have been a fully grown woman standing across from him, but Darius couldn't help feeling like he was staring into the determined pine-green eyes of the same little girl next door back then.

"I have never once asked for it, but you, Darius Williams, owe me a favor," she said, smile absolutely wiped clean. Her next words were spoken with a familiar resolve that gave him no space for a response. Not that he would have known what to say if he'd had the time to do so.

"My wedding is in an hour...and I need you to stop it."

A DEATH AT THE WEDDING

TYLER ANNE SNELL

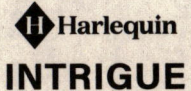

INTRIGUE

If you purchased this book without a cover you should be aware that this book is stolen property. It was reported as "unsold and destroyed" to the publisher, and neither the author nor the publisher has received any payment for this "stripped book."

This book is for Tyler, Dad, Mike, Hana, Damon and sometimes Brian. There was a lot going on when this book was written, but Core Group gave me the fun giggles I needed every night to start over fresh again in the morning. Thanks for the laughs, screams and inside jokes.

Harlequin®
INTRIGUE™

ISBN-13: 978-1-335-69056-2

A Death at the Wedding

Copyright © 2026 by Tyler Anne Snell

All rights reserved. No part of this book may be used or reproduced in any manner whatsoever without written permission.

Without limiting the exclusive rights of any author, contributor or the publisher of this publication, any unauthorized use of this publication to train generative artificial intelligence (AI) technologies is expressly prohibited. Harlequin also exercises their rights under Article 4(3) of the Digital Single Market Directive 2019/790 and expressly reserves this publication from the text and data mining exception.

This is a work of fiction. Names, characters, places and incidents are either the product of the author's imagination or are used fictitiously. Any resemblance to actual persons, living or dead, businesses, companies, events or locales is entirely coincidental.

For questions and comments about the quality of this book, please contact us at CustomerService@Harlequin.com.

TM and ® are trademarks of Harlequin Enterprises ULC.

Harlequin Enterprises ULC
22 Adelaide St. West, 41st Floor
Toronto, Ontario M5H 4E3, Canada
www.Harlequin.com

HarperCollins Publishers
Macken House, 39/40 Mayor Street Upper,
Dublin 1, D01 C9W8, Ireland
www.HarperCollins.com

Printed in Lithuania

Tyler Anne Snell lives in South Alabama with her same-named husband, their artist kiddo, four mini "lions" and a burning desire to meet Kurt Russell. Her superpowers include binge-watching TV and herding cats. When she isn't writing thrilling mysteries and romance, she's reading everything she can get her hands on. How she gets through each day starts and ends with a big cup of coffee. Visit her at tylerannesnell.com.

Books by Tyler Anne Snell

Harlequin Intrigue

Manhunt
Toxin Alert
Dangerous Recall

Small Town Last Stand

Search for the Truth
The Deputy's Secret Double
Against the Clock
A Death at the Wedding

The Saving Kelby Creek Series

Uncovering Small Town Secrets
Searching for Evidence
Surviving the Truth
Accidental Amnesia
Cold Case Captive
Retracing the Investigation

Visit the Author Profile page at Harlequin.com.

CAST OF CHARACTERS

Darius Williams—The loner detective always plays by the rules. Yet when he's reunited with the girl who saved his life all those years ago and her secrets, he finds himself breaking his own code. A small price to pay for keeping her safe.

Evelyn Myers—Coming back to Seven Roads to get married wasn't part of her secret plan, but running into the man who shares a scar with her was. She knows she can trust the boy next door. But will his badge get in the way?

Scott Keys—This powerful philanthropist has promised to help Seven Roads recover from the attacks it's been facing through the years, but his real intentions may be far more sinister.

Mitchell Keys—The younger brother of Scott Keys, his real relationship with Eve is a mystery.

Theo & Winnie—The adult children of some of the sheriff's department's finest, they stay by Darius's side as his helpful mentees.

Gary Whittaker—The Keyses' family lawyer, his murder spurs an investigation that forces Darius and Eve to team up.

Chapter One

Evelyn Myers wasn't book smart. She didn't have any school trophies or impressive college accolades. Her skills were average, her ability to solve math equations low, and to say she was uncoordinated was like saying it got dark at night. Eve wasn't a standout from the crowd. She was in it, trying to get from point A to point B while counting down the minutes until she could get home and take off her bra.

Her only notable exception, however, was enough to change absolutely everything for the worse.

Eve had a soft spot for trouble.

Which was why she was wearing a wedding dress beneath her coat and leaning against the McCoy County Sheriff Department's front desk with a smile that had been idling as long as Mrs. Jane had been trying to find the man she'd come calling for.

"Darius—I mean, Detective Williams is out on a call," Mrs. Jane said after she placed the phone back on its ancient cradle. It was as outdated as the interior of the building, but it wasn't like the small as small town of Seven Roads, Georgia, should have been expected to meet the current times with vigor.

Eve hadn't been back in town since she was twelve, and now at thirty-five she was sure as spit boiling on the sidewalk in summer that the dust on top of the vending machine in the lobby hadn't been cleaned since she had been living with her daddy in that old house on Maple.

"Do you know if he'll back anytime soon?" Eve asked. She subtly pulled her coat even tighter over a dress that cost more than her last apartment's rent. Mrs. Jane might not have recognized the little girl who had been a local all those years ago, but the wedding dress would be a dead giveaway to the fact that now she was Mrs. Keys-To-Be.

Eve Myers was unimpressive. But the family Eve Myers was marrying into had a net worth of almost half a billion dollars, spearheaded by the absolute stud of a bachelor named Scott Keys. Very impressive.

Even though she wasn't marrying Scott, she *was* marrying his little brother, Mitchell.

The running joke in the media was she was getting the keys to the castle, not the entire kingdom.

But standing there, staring at Mrs. Jane trying to find an excuse to shoo her away, Eve could tell she was as unimpressive to the woman as the frayed carpet beneath their feet.

"You'll just have to leave your name and number, sweetie," Mrs. Jane settled on, some spice to her Southern syrup. "That's the best I can do if you don't have an appointment with him already. He's a very busy man. He's the only detective in the county, you know."

Eve didn't need the Darius Williams who was a detective.

She needed the Darius Williams who owed her a favor.

Eve sighed out heavy. Her wedding dress sure was tight.

"Leaving all that isn't going to do me any good right now." She tapped the counter with her knuckle twice. "I'll see myself out now."

Mrs. Jane looked like she wanted to say something, but Eve's attention flitted to the giant analog clock above the double doors leading outside.

It was almost four o'clock.

Which meant five wasn't far behind.

An hour and a half until I get married. Eve growled out at herself. *You sure did make a mess of things, huh?*

If she had known this morning what she did now, she could have avoided this whole thing. Instead, Eve pressed out into the cold of a true rare Georgia winter. She was wondering if Darius still lived out on Maple—wondered if his mama had kept her promise—but knew even if she ran out there, he was working. Seeing the old house wouldn't do a dang thing other than help her reminisce.

Eve pulled her coat closer and chided herself for not being the kind of woman who came up with backup plans when a couple walking past caught her attention.

The man she didn't recognize, but his deputy's uniform read *Gavin.* The woman, at least a foot shorter and a pregnant belly wider, was dressed sharply in slacks, a sweater and a leather jacket. A badge was clipped onto her exposed belt, but Eve couldn't see any name on her. Not that she needed shiny metal to recognize Wildcard Rose Little. A town menace to some, a hero to many, especially over the last few years. No one messed with the petite woman without regretting it. The same had been just as true when they were in first grade and Danny Ripken had refused to let Rose on his dodgeball team during recess. He'd called her *too little, just like your name* and had laughed a whole lot at what he thought had been a Grade A insult.

Rose had given him a few moments with it before pegging him in the face with a rubber ball. His nose had busted like a mighty geyser, followed by giant crocodile tears. Rose hadn't been finished.

"Did that hurt, just a little?"

One question filled with a sea of sass.

It had been enough to get Rose picked first for teams in dodgeball after, and now years later, the memory had made it easy to spot the adult version of that small spitfire.

She rubbed at her pregnant belly and kept on, not at all recognizing Eve.

But Eve had locked in on the first mention of their only detective's name. The second mention came quickly after.

"Darius said they were headed back from the hospital with the paperwork for the request, but we all know it's going to be a pain in the backside. Last time…"

Rose's words trailed away as she and Deputy Gavin made it to the department's front steps. Their retreating backs took the hope that had been snuffed out by Mrs. Jane and fanned it back to life.

The hospital.

Lane Medical.

With only one road connecting it to Seven Roads.

Eve jumped into her hatchback and was off in a flash toward County Road 22.

If she'd had a phone, if she'd had his number now, if she knew without a doubt that he wouldn't hang up on her the second she asked—

Eve growled out in frustration again.

The only chance she had was to look Darius Williams right in the eye and remind him of one old, simple truth.

Darius was hers.

And she needed his help.

The second Eve was on County 22, she pressed the gas pedal to the floorboard.

Chapter Two

Darius Williams was late getting on the road because, despite years of working relatively solo, he had begrudgingly taken on not one but *two* busybodies under his worn, tired and slightly annoyed wings.

Annoyed, not because they were a handful by themselves.

No. Annoyed because Oil was sitting in the back seat and arguing with Water in the passenger's seat.

The water portion of the problematic duo was sitting shotgun and rolling her eyes. She had a notebook open on her lap, notes neatly written out in tight rows and a fancy book bag at her feet. Winnie Collins, the little girl that the McCoy County Sheriff's Department had watched grow up alongside her young and extremely talkative father, Price, through the years.

Now she was about to graduate college, a budding professional in a pantsuit and a shocking reminder that time did indeed go fast when you weren't paying attention.

Though Darius couldn't help but see the preteen in her at the added huff she sent toward the oil portion of the duo in the back seat.

Darius hadn't watched Theo Weaver grow up, but he had caught the tail end of his teenager years after the sheriff had taken him in. Now he was a year out of college and had been officially adopted by the Weaver brood.

Which meant that Darius had somehow gone from the only detective in the county to the only detective in the county who had been talked into helping the oldest children of the McCoy County Sheriff's Department's most beloved.

Some of the newer hires might have balked at the pressure.

Darius, thirty-six, no kids and single, simply wanted turn up the radio to drown out their bickering.

Instead, he kept quiet as Winnie went for another pound of flesh from Theo in the back seat.

"Listen, I'm not saying *you're* wrong," she said. "I'm just saying *I'm* right. So do you want to keep talking about it or just agree to move on with the facts?"

"The *facts*?" Theo repeated, voice pitching higher and not at all showing signs of moving on. Darius heard the resulting rustling of the laptop bag that had been constantly glued to the boy's side. "Do you need to see the data again? I have it all right here, in plain text *and* code. All you have are *feelings*."

"Feelings?" Winnie shot back. "You mean my *experiences* with other human beings? You know, those things you can't talk to without getting on every single one of their nerves?"

Darius finally made it out onto County Road 22, but he knew the ten-minute drive to the sheriff's department would be the end of him if he didn't stop the young'uns from slandering one another.

So he cleared his throat.

Despite their drive to prove the other wrong, both Winnie and Theo quieted in an instant. At times like this Darius didn't mind the reputation he had gotten as the stonehearted dealer of death, an extremely dramatic depiction of a homicide detective, if you asked him.

"Having both the feelings *and* facts when you're trying to answer a question isn't a bad thing," he said. "When I solve a case I look for evidence *and* the story that fills the spaces in between. The head and the heart. If you don't have one, there's no point in having the other."

"But we're not looking at a homicide case," Theo pointed out. "We're trying to figure out if the new pharmaceutical company is actually doing their jobs or not. That puts me neck-deep in data, and data doesn't need a story."

"Data *plus* interviews from the admin, former patients and staff who worked in the research annex where the drug study was taking place *creates* a story," Winnie returned just as quickly. "One you are, for whatever reason, ignoring because you think facts and figures are never, ever wrong."

Darius stifled a sigh. He hadn't solved the problem but instead thrown more fuel on the fire. He rolled his eyes to County 22 through the windshield.

Then that eye roll went to nothing but focused attention.

A little hatchback was parked on the shoulder of road, emergency lights on, and driver's-side door wide open. A woman was standing in the middle of the road, coat pulled tight around her.

"Look alive," he told the kids.

Darius wasn't in a cruiser, but he reached for the walkie-talkie that was always in his personal vehicle, just in case. He slowed, taking in the details as his passengers did the same but with volume. Their feud turned to joint observation in a snap.

"She doesn't look hurt," Theo said from the back seat. "No blood or open wounds. The vehicle seems to be in one piece. The tires aren't flat. At least not the ones I can see."

He was right. The hatchback was facing the same direction as traffic but from there didn't seem to be any obvious reason it was disabled.

"She doesn't look distressed either," Winnie added. "Maybe a little excited?"

Darius put down his radio.

He agreed.

The woman didn't look worried or hurt or even a bit stressed.

She did, however, look familiar.

It was an odd feeling that pressed against Darius as he put on his hazards and pulled over onto the side of the road.

Seven Roads was a small town; McCoy County was bigger, but the faces rarely changed. He had been a career local, born to a woman born to the town, and had rarely left the county limits since. Where they were now wasn't exactly a hot spot of tourism or even a well-traveled road from simple passers-through.

Maybe she was a relative or friend visiting?

Maybe she was new to town?

Maybe she was just lost.

Either way she wasn't missing an inch of him. Her stare burrowed into him as he pulled to the shoulder.

Then she smiled.

Darius hesitated for the briefest of moments. That smile? It…

The woman started toward them, her pace obviously slower than the easy-to-see excitement spreading through her.

Darius left the engine running and handed the walkie-talkie to Winnie. The girl took it but threw out one last observation before he had the door open.

"She's wearing a wedding dress!"

The woman's steps were slow, but her coat fell open at

the movement. She didn't try to cover herself back up as the white fabric became unmistakable against the backdrop of the old county road.

Why would a woman wearing a wedding dress be in the middle of County 22?

"Stay here."

Winnie and Theo were quiet as Darius left the warmth of vehicle for the crisp cold of the Georgia winter. It would turn his nose red if he stayed out in it for more than a few minutes. The woman had to have been waiting for a bit: her nose was red as she approached him.

That didn't seem to dull her excitement.

She stopped a few feet short and put her hands on her hips. The smile of excitement switched to an undeniable mischievousness in a flash.

"Well, if it isn't Darius Williams." She tilted her head to the side. "I was getting a little worried you'd somehow found a new way back to town since I've been gone."

His brow rose in question.

The woman seemed to be in her own world. Her gaze swept up from his feet to his eyes.

"I can tell you for sure the one thing that changed is how tall you are," she continued. "You outgrew me by almost a foot. Not sure if I like that, to be honest."

Darius had been the only detective in McCoy County for years. He hadn't seen a lot of things compared to bigger counties or cities—nothing that had left him speechless or staggering, at least—and even outside of work his surprises, scares and startles hadn't been much at all. Nothing to write home about. Nothing to flip, rock or shake his world.

He could take a hit.

He could dole one out too.

He could button up his emotions, and he could unleash hell, if need be.

Even walking up to a woman waving him down in a wedding dress wasn't enough to move the needle on his radar from *cautious* to *confused*.

But then the stranger moved her hand up above her head to emphasize how he was taller.

And that's how he saw the small scar along the side of it.

It instantly reminded him of the scar on his back, jagged and uneven. Darker than his olive skin color and easy to spot if he wasn't careful with the sleeves of his shirt.

If the location were different, it would almost look like they had tried to match—

Darius's eyes flashed to the woman's face.

At first the woman had been nothing but average. Nice-looking in a pleasant, fine way. Green eyes, brunette. Hairstyle that might be expected for a wedding and a smile that was all right. A woman who might not stop traffic but could stop one driver.

But now?

Darius saw something else entirely.

Someone else.

The scar seemed to be the secret password to unlocking an entirely new version of the woman standing in the road, wearing a wedding dress.

"Evie?"

The name came out of his mouth on reflex.

"I guess some things always look the same no matter how long it's been." She nodded and then dropped her hand with a little shake. Like it was the most normal interaction in the world, she continued with a smile still. "Though, I guess you might not have figured it out had I been in a crowd. So I'm not sure this counts all that much."

Her shoulders tightened, and her smile disappeared, all before Darius could mumble out a word in response. She tucked her hand and its scar into one of her coat pockets.

The scar that matched Darius's.

The scar that had changed his life.

The scar that would have been much worse had a little girl named Evelyn Myers not protected him with everything she had.

Now, scar out of sight, there might have been a fully grown woman standing across from him, but Darius couldn't help but feel like he was staring into the determined pine-green eyes of the same little girl next door back then.

"I have never once asked for it but, you, Darius Williams, owe me a favor," she said, smile absolutely wiped clean. Her next words were spoken with a familiar resolve that gave him no space for a response. Not that he would have known what to say if he'd had the time to do so.

"My wedding is in an hour…and I need you to stop it."

Chapter Three

There was something to be said for the passage of time. One day there was a gangly boy, subconscious and a little too quiet—wearing clothes that were a little too big—and the next there was a man standing in the place of his memory. Not completely unfamiliar, but absolutely not the same small boy Eve had met in the space between their houses when she was just as young.

Time hadn't paused because Eve had left.

Instead, it had built a boy into a man.

And it had apparently taken care to make that man quite the looker.

Darius Williams was one heck of a sight. There were no two ways about that. Built like a capital T, his upper body was wrapped in a button-up and corduroy jacket that fit him like a glove, and his Levi jeans hugged him right comfortable like an old friend. There wasn't a scrap of fabric on him that didn't fit him. Not an inch of awkward to see. In fact, Eve couldn't help but think if Darius ever wanted to leave the life of law enforcement behind, then he could make one heck of a living out of modeling denim for the masses.

It was obvious that he worked out or ate right or a little of both, she had decided as he'd walked across the asphalt to meet her.

And that was to speak nothing of the f
face of his was. Eve could see the boy she us
the coloring of his dark eyes and the overly
his matching brow, but the rest had taken to growing up
mighty fine. His jaw competed with the seriousness of his
expression—hard and slightly intimidating—and he had
undoubtedly grown into his nose. Though, it looked like it
might have been broken in the time since Eve had seen it
last. There was also a small scar at the top of his lip, barely
noticeable but there all the same.

Eve saw it with ease before he had even stopped across
from her.

Its corners never pulled up from its frown.

She had started to mentally comment on the slight wave
of his dark hair—and how it, too, was a far cry from the
buzz cut he'd been forced to keep as a kid—when a new
reality had hit her beneath the smile she couldn't help but
give when seeing him after all these years.

Darius hadn't recognized her.

Only after she had mentioned his height had she seen
the connections start to form.

If she had had more time, Eve would have smarted at
that. It wasn't like she had changed all that much since her
preteen years. Her hair was still just as middle-of-the-road
brown as it had been then. Her eyes, a muddling hazel. A
few freckles, a jawline that was nowhere near as cutting and
eyebrows that still rarely pulled together with such severity.
While she had been cute when she was a kid, that cuteness
had only grown into ordinary as an adult. It was, after all,
one reason the gossip had been wholly unkind to her once
it had been announced that she, an average woman on all
fronts, was marrying into the Keys family.

Still, Eve couldn't help but feel a little sting at being overlooked by him.

But there was a time and place to think longer on such things, and as the wind bit into the skin above the cut of her wedding dress, Eve reminded herself that now certainly wasn't it.

Her last words still hung heavy in the air between them.

"My wedding is in an hour…and I need you to stop it."

Darius looked just as serious as before, if only a bit confused on top of that.

He finally responded, but it was only one word.

"What?"

Eve reined in all thoughts of the little boy whose voice had never been that strong and barreled into her bottom line.

"I'm marrying Mitchell Keys at the old library downtown at five thirty," she said. "The wedding planner acts like we're an army unit going to war, so I'm sure that's a hard five thirty, and even if I try to stall she'll find a way to cut my metaphorical legs off. So if you can't get there before and find a reason to stop it from starting, then you have until five fifty to do something. After that we're saying *I do* and being told to awkwardly kiss in front of everyone."

Darius was wearing a watch. Eve went for it. He was faster and batted her hand away.

"I'm sorry but I'm going to need more than that," he said, holding his wrist up and away.

Eve still tilted her head to see the face of the watch. The minute hand was a little too close to the two.

She had wasted more time than she had thought waiting for Darius to show up.

"There's not enough time to get into specifics. I just need the wedding to stop." She also needed to leave. The drive back would eat up at least ten minutes. She was already playing way too close to the line.

Darius didn't understand, and although she knew that was a valid reaction, that didn't mean knowing fixed the issue.

"Why don't you just stop your own wedding?" Darius's expression hardened ever so slightly. "Unless you're being forced to go through with it?"

Eve could understand that worry with the Keys family involved—what couldn't a family so wealthy get away with?—but this problem was solely hers.

"I'm not being forced, but I can't stop it myself." Eve grabbed his wrist to steady her gaze at his watch. Darius let her this time. She indeed had read it right originally.

Which meant she had to leave.

Now.

"Why not? What's going on, Evelyn?"

She didn't like the use of her full name, but Eve let his wrist go and took a step back.

"I don't care what you do to stop it, but please don't let anyone know that I asked you to do it." Eve watched as confusion washed over Darius's face. She didn't have time to explain so she reiterated the only point she had to convince him. "You do this and we're even, Darius."

Eve turned so quickly that her coat slapped closed against her chest. She didn't wait to see what his next move was. She didn't look back at him at all, in fact, as she started her engine and got back onto County. For the second time that day she pushed the gas pedal all the way down.

THERE WAS A road that was old, weathered and worn that only a few locals knew about. Most of those called it the Twig.

Just take the Twig, they might say. *If it's dry out and your tires are fine, use the Twig to shave off some time.*

Darius's tires and truck were fine—it paid that the department had their very own on-call mechanic in Rose's husband—and the rain hadn't been coming all that much since the cold snap had snapped at them in the last week. Taking the Twig from County wouldn't get him stranded or find him in any inconvenience. It would simply take him from the big road to the mouth of Harper's Hill, a neighborhood that was a hop, skip and a jump away from the church on Main's parking lot.

Which just so happened to be across the way from the building that had once housed the Seven Roads Library.

Darius tightened his grip around the steering wheel. He hadn't moved the truck an inch since watching Eve drive off. The kids in his car hadn't moved either. Only their mouths had gone to work and, to be fair, each question had been valid.

"What's going on? What did she say? Where is she going? Are we following?" Theo's questions had come out in short, consistent bursts, concerned about the current situation and what came next.

Winnie had been more people-oriented in her queries.

"Do you know her? Are you all right?" she had asked on the boy's heels.

Darius hadn't yet answered anyone. Instead, since sitting back in the driver's seat, he had been doing everything in his power to calm down.

Evelyn Myers was back.

Evelyn Myers *was back.*

And she was getting married.

Darius felt his own jaw start to ache. He let his too-tight grip on the steering wheel go and rubbed a thumb beneath his chin.

You, Darius Williams, owe me a favor.

He did. He really did.

Darius checked his mirrors and pulled onto County. He didn't answer either kid's question. Instead, he flipped the script.

"What do you two know about a wedding going on today in town today?" he asked.

Theo was fast with a reply.

"The younger Keys brother is getting married, and the entire town is blowing it out of proportion. Wait. Was that the bride?"

Darius nodded toward Winnie. She didn't miss the direction.

"It's a big deal because Scott Keys is the groom's brother."

"Scott Keys," Darius repeated. The name was familiar, but he couldn't place it.

Winnie helped him out.

"He's known as the White Knight of Small-town Living," she started. "He finds ways to invest or bring in jobs that help rebuild more rural, forgotten or failing small towns. He had a few interviews at the steel mill here before he announced that his brother would be getting married in Seven Roads. Nothing's been confirmed, but the hope is that he's about to white-knight Seven Roads."

"But it's his brother getting married, Mitchell?"

That name wasn't at all familiar.

Regardless, Darius didn't like it.

Out of his periphery, he saw Winnie nod.

"He doesn't have a fun nickname or really any kind of popularity other than being called Scott Keys's brother. His media presence, at least, is pretty low."

"My bet is that his wedding wouldn't be that big of a deal if he wasn't marrying the White Knight's assistant," Theo tacked on.

"She's Scott Keys's assistant?" Darius asked.

There was a small silence. He bet the two kids shared a look.

"The bride-to-be is, yeah," Winnie answered after the moment. "She used to be a local... Is that how you know her? From when she lived here as a kid?"

Darius nodded, but even he knew it was tight.

"She was my neighbor."

Theo made a noise. Out of his periphery, Darius saw Winnie swat back at Theo.

"So that *was* her just now?" he asked. "What did she want? Was she waiting for you? Is there something between—"

"Theo," Winnie hissed.

"What? Don't act like you weren't asking me a billion questions while he was out there talking to her—"

Darius saw it up ahead and to the left. If you didn't know it was there, it would be easy to drive by. He glanced at the truck's clock.

If he wanted to get to the old library in time, the Twig was his only option.

But did that mean he was actually going to—

"Son of a—" Darius turned the wheel and bumped along into the Twig. Whatever Winnie and Theo were arguing about, they stopped.

"What are you doing?" Theo asked, but Winnie proved that she was less analytical than the boy. She had already made the jump to the more human problem of the equation.

"Are we going to the wedding?"

Darius cussed a good cuss.

"No," he decided. "We're not."

Despite good tires and an engine that could move mountains, the Twig bounced them good and dirty as he continued driving it.

"Well, we sure aren't going to the department this way," Theo pointed out.

Darius was growing hot under the collar. Bothered every bump and divot they drove over, annoyance growing like the clouds of sand his tires kicked up into the air.

Theo was right. He was heading in the opposite direction.

He cussed low again.

It wasn't like hiding it from them would do him any good. Darius was out of time to do anything other than floor it to the library. Plus, he couldn't just drop them off on the side of the road. Not only had he promised to watch out for the two, it just wasn't good policy to ditch the sheriff's son and one of their star deputy's daughters on the side of the road.

Though, for a moment, Darius did entertain the idea.

He would have preferred not to have an audience for what he couldn't believe he was entertaining.

"We're going to the wedding," he finally caved.

"Oh, so the bride just invited you," Theo guessed.

Darius tilted his head a little, trying to figure out exactly how to say what he needed to—and exactly what it was that he himself intended to do.

Without wanting to, he recalled the distinct smell of blood. So strong he had to fight the urge to touch the scar on his back.

He wasn't in that room anymore.

He wasn't that kid anymore.

There was no blade, no blood and no terror gripping his chest so tight he could barely breathe.

There was no girl with her arms around him, bleeding too, but not at all scared.

Yet, even though he wasn't thirteen anymore, there was the smell of blood filling his nose.

But, then, there was also bubble gum.

Faint but still a memory that had endured over the years.

The anger in Darius, the frustration and confusion, the feeling he couldn't quite define, floated away.

He took a deep breath.

Then he let it out.

"We're not going to watch the wedding," he told his passengers. "We're going to stop it."

Chapter Four

If Eve were being honest with herself, she hadn't spent much time in her youth imagining her future wedding, and the few bouts of fancy she had given herself as a kid had only ever gone one way.

Something small in the backyard, daisies and a sunflower or two around an arch her dad built, and some of those nice folding white chairs she had seen at Mrs. Dunphy's garage sale pushed in between her old refrigerator and the electoral box in the wall, sitting pretty on the lawn. There wouldn't be a lot of people there—of her own family, all she needed was her dad anyways—but there would be enough that they would have to buy a party platter from the home-cooking restaurant on Main for the reception.

Eve would wear some pretty white dress that poofed at the bottom and maybe put her hair up some nice-looking way. She'd paint her nails blue to match her groom's tie.

The groom, of course, would be the boy next door.

A little nervous but smiling wide like he did when they were watching movies or sneaking out to the Becker Farm's creek or passing notes between their windows.

Eve would walk down the aisle toward Darius without an ounce of hesitation because their wedding was inevitable. She *had*, after all, made it very clear that he was hers for life, and wasn't that just another way to say *husband and wife*?

Now, though, reality showed Eve something quite different.

She wasn't strolling down the grass aisle of her backyard, arm looped around her father's, with sunflowers and daisies and a few guests in attendance. There was no poof to her tight designer dress. Her nails weren't painted a fun blue, and the groom certainly wasn't Darius Williams.

The Seven Roads Library had suffered a fire in the early nineties, and while it been repaired since, the main room no longer resembled its former glory. Instead of a large room filled with shelves and books and a librarian's desk, there was an expansive space surrounded by exposed brick, laid out in refurbished hardwoods, and a partially domed ceiling of glass.

The sunlight poured through that ceiling and made a design in shadows against a wooden arch at the end of the room. One that had *not* been custom-made by her dad but instead bought with Keys money.

The same Keys money that had the once-big room now feeling claustrophobic. They might have been in Seven Roads, not exactly the prime spot for upscale socializing, but almost every suit and dress in attendance had made the trip without fuss.

And they weren't there for the man in the tux Eve was walking toward.

No, they were there for the man at his side, movie-star smile warming an already-attractive face.

Scott Keys.

The White Knight.

Always wrapped in philanthropist glory, something designer and charm.

Everyone wanted him; some wanted to be him.

Eve wanted to destroy him.

And so did the man standing next to the altar.

Eve smiled at Mitchell as the wedding march ended. He met her at the one step up in the room, holding his arm out. He wasn't unattractive, but it was hard to see what made him shine while constantly being in his brother's shadow.

He had blue eyes that looked nice with his tan and obediently straight brown hair, while his fashion sense felt more natural than showy. When they had first met he had been wearing earrings in both ears and a bomber jacket that had felt extremely stylish. But that had felt like a lifetime ago.

Now, even at his own wedding, he wore a tuxedo that visibly paled in comparison to his brother's.

His eyes, though, they were kind as they took her in.

"You look beautiful, Evelyn," he whispered. She took his arm as she nodded to the compliment.

"You're pretty snazzy too," she returned.

A smile flashed across his face, not at all the same one he'd been wearing a moment ago. A genuine one of appreciation.

Not romantic love.

Because, even though they were both there of their own accord, neither one of them had actually planned on getting this far. Their plan had only included the ruse of dating, of getting engaged, not wedding bells and library chapels.

That had been Scott's idea.

"Family is the most important thing in this world," he'd told them, holding out his mother's ring to Mitchell. "It's the greatest wealth you can attain, so why not go ahead and become wealthier?"

Mitchell had had no choice to propose then—another part of his life taken over by his brother.

Six months later, and the memory still made Eve's blood start to boil.

Scott Keys was a man standing on a pedestal of his own making.

And she desperately wanted to knock him off it.

Mitchell's smile tightened as they stopped at their designated spots across from the man who had been ordained, hired and picked by Scott. He squeezed her arm once before letting go.

Eve understood that quick grip.

He wanted to know if they were really going to go through with the wedding. If she had managed to find the solution to their problem. If wherever she had snuck out to and gone that afternoon had borne any fruit, so to speak.

The man between them asked them to face one another.

Eve used the time to glance back down the aisle and at the double doors she had just walked through.

She didn't want divine intervention to stop their sham marriage.

She wanted Darius Williams to bust through those doors.

Eve mentally sighed.

How dramatic would that have been? she thought. Seeing Darius bust through those doors yelling "I object!"

It would make everything seem like a movie and earn Eve a chance to escape the problem that she had, in part, created.

Darius, however, didn't burst through the doors, and she turned around to listen to the officiant. The part where someone could object came and went without a peep. The vows came next, and Mitchell—not one given to public speaking like his brother—struggled through his.

Eve kept smiling through it all, even though the hope that Darius would show up was starting to fade.

Had she been too nostalgic? Had the request been too outrageous? Had their past stayed firmly rooted in the past?

Despite herself, Eve started to think about what happened next.

The honeymoon.

For completely different reasons, it made her blood run cold.

She resisted the urge to look over Mitchell's shoulder. His brother would also still be, no doubt, smiling too.

Neither one of them meant it.

"Now, Evelyn, it's time to read your vows." The officiant's voice sliced through her thoughts like a machete through butter. While there were many things that affected others, Eve had always had a way of going with the flow. Sadness, fear, anger…they rolled off her shoulders like water, and she just kept going.

But now, there was a coldness in her stomach that was starting to spread.

She shouldn't have let it get this far. She shouldn't have—

A loud bang sounded through the main room. Mitchell jumped, while a flurry of gasps and mutterings sprang from the guests. Eve, though, whipped her head around to look at the double doors.

The coldness in her warmed in an instant.

The doors were closing and standing in front of them was the little boy who owed her a favor.

Darius.

He'd come, and just in time too.

Eve was wondering how he would play the next part when the door opened again.

It was a man she didn't recognize. The star-shaped badge at his hip, however, was easy to see even from her spot at the altar.

The sheriff of McCoy County had a tight smile.

Darius wasn't smiling at all.

"When I said stop the wedding at all costs, this isn't what I had in mind."

Eve's voice was small, but there was no shake or tremor to it. All things considered, it was impressive. Not many could see a dead body and manage some humor.

They were standing next to the mouth of a small hallway that fed from the old library's main lobby and into the area that used to house offices and the break room. The wedding party was spread between those rooms now. Mitchell Keys was in the break room with his brother.

A man wearing a gray suit was dead on the bench seat next to the closed double doors a few feet from them.

Eve cut her gaze away from the man and back to Darius. Again, he felt impressed at her composure. Then again, maybe it wasn't all that surprising. This was Evelyn Myers, after all. Even as a kid she'd had a habit of not blanching.

"His name is Gary Whittaker," she said, voice back to a normal volume. "He's the Keyses' family lawyer. Or was, I guess."

Darius had a pad of paper out, a pen in his other hand, but he didn't write anything down. Like the young Eve had had a habit of not swerving at whatever game of chicken she had been forced into, the young Darius also had his own habit of remembering everything the girl said.

He suspected time hadn't changed that ingrained skill.

Still, for appearance's sake, he held on to both.

"Family lawyer, huh?" he said. "Pretty close, I guess, to come to an out-of-town wedding."

Eve shrugged.

"When you have enough money, even the lawyers get

close enough to become part of the family. He was at almost just as many family events as I was."

"So you were friends?"

Darius didn't have to look back at the body to know the details. Once he had rushed into the lobby and noticed the man, it had been hard not to take it all in.

A man who appeared to be in his late fifties, early sixties, slumped over on a worn and weathered wooden bench. Not at all worn and weathered was his suit, charcoal gray, with a white button-up shirt beneath it. The white was pristine in all places except where it had come untucked at his waist. It was stained crimson.

The bullet wound that had most likely killed him was hidden beneath his coat.

For Eve, not much had changed about her appearance since Darius had seen her at County 22. Her coat was gone, and her hair had been pinned up. Another quick look down at her dress, and Darius couldn't help but think that the Eve of their younger years would have disliked such an uncomfortably tight thing.

He buttoned that line of thought as Eve sighed out long.

"I wouldn't call us *friends*, but we were familiar," she said. "As Scott Keys's personal assistant, I had more cause to run into him than most. Especially since he helped out with the philanthropy side of things."

She shook her head—not even a strand of hair moved.

"I don't know why anyone would want to kill him, though. Or why they would kill him and then put him here."

She motioned toward the late Gary Whittaker.

"And before you ask how I know he was killed somewhere else and then moved after, it's because there's not more blood," she added. "If anyone other than you had found him, they might not even have noticed he'd been shot at all."

She was right.

There was no blood around the victim. Not even a drop.

He had been shot elsewhere and moved.

But why?

"When's the last time you talked to or saw Mr. Whittaker?" Darius asked.

He had to raise his voice a little to compensate for the chatter taking place across the room from them. The county coroner, Martin Blues, a newly hired crime scene investigator, and Deputy Gavin were professional when it came to their jobs. They were also social about it too. Darius had already had to skirt Martin on two other cases after the younger man had tried talking sports over a dead body. He understood trying to bring brevity into a heavy situation, but even the less-than-social Darius knew there was a time and a place.

Eve didn't seem to mind the new distraction. Her brow furrowed, and her frown deepened.

"The last time I saw Gary was back at the company."

"In Atlanta?"

She nodded.

"Scott had a meeting with a Green Suit and asked Gary to sit in. I didn't sit with them but ended up walking Gary to his car in the parking garage. He talked about the upcoming wedding and *his* wedding to his now ex-wife, but it was all just small talk."

Darius tilted his head to the side a little.

"*Green Suit?*" he asked. "Is that some kind of business term I'm not familiar with?"

Darius had the distinct impression that Eve almost rolled her eyes at that but held it in.

"Green Suits are what I secretly call the businessmen who don't mind donating or investing big money to the Keys Foundation but, for whatever reason, don't like a little ol' assistant like me being in the room." She already had her arms crossed over her chest, but Darius noticed she tightened the stance. "It's the only time I'm okay with being a little passive-aggressive."

One of the office doors behind them opened. Darius kept his spot next to Eve but angled around to see whose heavy footsteps were headed their way.

It wasn't long before the sheriff's long face was staring right at him.

"Miss Myers, if you would excuse us for a moment, I need to have a talk with Detective Williams."

Sheriff Liam Weaver was a large, solid man of muscle and steel, but when he needed to cut his ingrained intimidation down, the smile his wife had helped him find over the years did the trick. His long face softened with the small upturn of his lips as he told Eve she could return to the wedding party.

Eve glanced at Darius but nodded and left without another word.

No sooner than he heard one of the doors shut behind them than the sheriff's smile all but disappeared.

"The talk with Scott Keys went that well?" Darius asked.

Liam's jaw tightened for a moment.

"He's not the Keys brother I'm worried about," he said after a moment. His already-low voice grumbled lower. "What all do you know about Mitchell Keys?"

That surprised Darius.

He answered with honesty.

"Only what the kids told me earlier. He's the younger, unpopular one of the two."

And Eve's future husband.

"Why?" Darius added.

Liam glanced across the room. Martin seemed to be done with his initial pass. Darius would talk to him next, then go from there. Starting with retracing the man's steps and hopefully finding where he'd been killed. Then he would—

"I think Mitchell Keys might be our killer," Liam said, halting all of Darius's future plans in an instant.

"What?"

The sheriff sighed. He wasn't looking at Darius when he explained. Which was good, because Darius's usual composure momentarily cracked at what he said next.

"And I think there's a good possibility that the bride-to-be might have helped him do it."

Chapter Five

Eve was happy to get out of her wedding dress and slip back into more comfortable clothes. The slightly oversize knit sweater hung past the waist of her jeans while her tennis shoes felt like an apology to her poor feet. She had never been a heels type of girl, and yet she'd had to endure the tall traps she had promptly thrown back into her bag once she had entered the bridal party dressing room. The bobby pins forcing her hair into a headache-inducing tight hold were more of a production to get rid of. She only managed to pull half of them out before deciding the ones on top could stay until the last vestiges of adrenaline had disappeared. Because, ever since seeing Gary slumped over in the lobby, dead, Eve had felt like ants were crawling beneath her skin.

She felt for Gary. And she worried for her plan.

Not to mention the Darius of it all. After he and the sheriff had interrupted the wedding, she had believed a wonderful excuse was coming her way—something that would put a hiccup large enough in the proceedings that she would have more time to do what she needed.

But a murder?

That hadn't been even remotely on her list of possibilities.

A knock on the suite door sounded. Eve checked her reflection in the mirror to make sure she didn't look as chaotic as she felt and scooped up her bag. No matter who was at the door, she had already decided that she wouldn't be going back to the old library anytime soon. Especially not for her own wedding.

A familiar and not-at-all-liked face was frowning so severely that Eve had to fight the impulsive urge to shut the door as soon as she had opened it.

Maria Sanderson was a few years younger than Eve but acted as if she had lived twenty more lives than her at any given moment. Her confidence came from two places and two places only: her husband's money, and a lifetime of having everything she wanted handed to her. It was a slightly harsh assessment that Eve had made after meeting the wife of Scott Keys's best friend, Toby. But now, a year later, she stood steadfast in her opinion.

Maria had never liked a pragmatic, daily worker like Eve. The gossip that came with Eve, though? That was worth more than any friendship.

Maria was already talking the moment the door opened.

"I can't believe someone died at your wedding!" Maria followed Eve out of the room and down the hallway. She was still in her designer dress and covered in various accessories that sparkled even under the library's old fluorescent lights. Eve didn't miss the woman's gaze down at her now very underwhelmingly average outfit. On a normal day it would have most likely prompted a backhanded compliment of some sort. Today, however, Maria hurried past any veiled or not-so-veiled insult.

"Well, I guess calling it a wedding is generous, all things considered," she said. "The ceremony didn't even finish, and I'm guessing that rescheduling for later tonight isn't in the cards either, huh?"

Maria might have liked gossip, but she wasn't giving Eve

any space to provide a word. Her heels clicked and echoed through the hallway around them.

"The sheriff already told us all to go back to the hotel," she continued. "Toby already left to talk to management about extending our stay. He wanted to go with the sheriff and Scott to Gary's room to look around, but I told him we should probably take care of the guests who didn't want to stay here more than a day, you know? Just in case they're needed with the investigation."

While Maria had been talking, Eve had been inching them toward the library's lobby. Pointing out that a man's death was more important than a guest's potential discomfort didn't seem the right play, though Eve felt the urge to say it all the same. But unlike Maria, she knew there was a time and place for things.

Right now? All Eve wanted to do was talk to only two people. Maria was neither one of those people.

Still, Eve couldn't deny she was glad for the mini-update on what had happened in the time she had been sequestered to the bridal party dressing room to change.

Namely, finding where one of the two people she wanted to see next had gone.

"Is Mitchell with Scott and the sheriff?" Eve asked. "I can't get him on the phone."

Maria's eyes widened. Her lipstick's deep red looked oddly off-putting. The fluorescent lights really weren't doing anyone favors here.

"He's probably at the police station or department or whatever it's called. I saw him leave, but he got into a police car with some man in a uniform."

Eve paused in her short stride.

"He left in one of their cars?"

Maria nodded.

"Don't worry. He was sitting in the front seat, or else I would have said something, believe you me."

Why had Mitchell gotten into a deputy's cruiser at all? Why hadn't he gone with Scott and the sheriff?

Eve felt her brow knit together. Maria noticed but didn't understand the emotion behind it.

The diamond of her wedding ring had swiveled downward. It pinched a little as she patted Eve's shoulder.

"Don't you worry, I'll be talking to Toby and Scott about getting you two married as soon as possible so we can get back to civilization."

Eve didn't have the mental space to point out that Maria had just insulted her hometown and, instead, finally made her way out into the lobby.

After waiting in the offices for half an hour, then escaping to change, the old library's lobby had apparently been emptied. Gary's body was gone, and in its place some caution tape and a sign had been put up. All personnel and law enforcement were gone.

All but one.

Maria let out a little breath as both women saw Darius. There was definitely no denying he had more than grown up. Leaning against the wall next to one of the open front doors, he looked like he had stepped out of a magazine. Modeling denim, Eve couldn't help but think quick.

Maria must have also appreciated the sight.

When Darius pushed off the wall and came toward them, she cleared her throat ever so slightly. Then that too-dark lipstick moved into a sharklike smile.

Darius gave her a small nod, but his gaze didn't move from Eve. Which was good, considering he was one of the two people she was hoping to talk to now.

"Mrs. Keys, I was wondering if you wouldn't mind coming with me for a statement at the department?" He sure looked like Darius, but the voice and name change certainly threw Eve for a mental loop. She felt her brow fly high in question.

Maria beat her to a response.

"Miss Myers, actually," she corrected. "Sadly, the ceremony was cut short, so she's still Myers. Miss Myers."

This time, Darius looked her way. He didn't smile but did step back to open one of the doors even more wide.

"Even more of a reason to get going." He motioned for Eve to go through the door. She gladly accepted the directive.

"I'll be going now, Maria. Let me know if anything else happens, okay?"

Maria wasn't used to being brushed off, and normally Eve would have been more polite with it, but given the circumstances, she assumed the faux pas would be overlooked.

Darius, however, addressed Maria's presence the second they were in his truck.

"I don't like her," he said, grabbing at his seat belt. Eve followed suit but added in a snort.

"If you showed her your bank statements, she wouldn't like you either."

Darius made a sound of mock pain.

"Way to leg-sweep me there, Eve."

Eve didn't scramble for any kind of apology.

"Scott Keys might be *rich* rich, but Maria is married to his best friend Toby. And Toby? Already had six figures in his bank account before he exited the womb."

Not that Maria was much different. While she wasn't the stereotypical trust-fund baby, her mother had married a business tycoon in Texas. As far as Eve knew, neither woman had wanted for a thing after that.

Darius started the engine and had them aimed out of

the parking lot, all while shifting expressions. His obvious distaste for Maria's attitude smoothed a frown into a neutral middle expression.

"If you're not a fan either, why was she one of your bridesmaids? Or, I guess, *maid of honor*."

That surprised Eve.

"I guess you're still good at the details," she said. "I didn't think there was time to look around before you and the sheriff shut everything down."

In fact, other than a quick look between Eve and Darius while they were on opposite sides of the aisle, Darius hadn't met her gaze again until they were each pulled out of the offices to talk.

"Just because I was stopping your wedding didn't mean I wasn't paying attention."

His tone was as matter-as-fact as they came. It bothered Eve.

Part of her had expected him to show up, part of her knew it had been a ridiculous request. Regardless, shouldn't he have been asking more questions?

Even without poor Gary's death, she would have expected more than inquires about Maria Sanderson.

But who was she to nitpick?

"When Scott realized I wasn't planning on having any bridesmaids, he thought it would be a good to ask Maria since she loves big, social events. Janice and Renee, the bridesmaids, are from the foundation."

"The foundation? You mean the Keys Foundation?"

Eve nodded.

"So you work with them, then."

"Yes. Coworkers."

They were driving across Main Street. Eve didn't take in the scenery. She knew Seven Roads had changed; she didn't need to know how much. What she had to do next was too important for her to worry about the outside world.

Even when it came to Darius.

"When can I see Mitchell? I haven't been able to talk to him since you pulled me out to talk earlier."

"We're going to him right now."

His neutral tone pricked a little.

Eve looked sidelong at him.

"I heard that Scott was helping the sheriff. Did they find something? Do you know what happened to Gary?"

Darius didn't look her way, even as they slowed to a stop at a red light.

"We're working a lead right now."

Eve waited for more.

She didn't get it.

"What's the lead?"

Darius kept his eyes right on the road. The badge on the chain around his neck still shone in the fading sunlight.

For the first time since being back in Seven Roads, Eve saw the boy next door for what he was now.

A man of the law.

And, she realized too late, that his offer to take her to the department might not have had anything to do with their past at all.

"Darius, what's the lead?"

In profile she watched him clench his jaw. It took a moment for him to answer.

And it wasn't even an answer at all.

"Let's wait until we're at the department."

IT WAS HARD to tell who was the most unhappy in the room. There was Liam with his thumbs hooked into his belt loops, brows drawn in and lips thin, standing at the head of the meeting room table. His chair was empty behind him. He didn't seem like he was going to use it anytime soon.

Price wasn't as robust in his aggravation. He had come into the room and sat down at his usual spot next to Rose. Despite her promotion, she looked more at ease next to the deputy, like old times. One hand was on her belly, the other was balled on top of the table.

Deputy Gavin, usually quiet, sat across from Darius with a frown.

The sheriff spoke first.

"I know we've been through a lot of tricky cases over the last few years, but I have to point out that this one is a bit more complicated than I would like. And we need to make sure we keep everything—*everything*—aboveboard. No breaking the rules for the greater good. No going rogue. No missed check-ins because we're all friends here. Got it?"

He pressed his fingertips down onto the tabletop but let his gaze sweep over each of them until everyone had nodded.

Darius also dipped his chin too.

Liam didn't seem as convinced. Still, he moved on.

"As of right now we still haven't found where Gary Whittaker was killed, but according to Doc Ernest, the cause of death was from the shot to his gut. Wherever he was before, he bled a lot. That's where I need you two to use your powers that come with being long-time locals." The sheriff motioned to Rose and Price. Even though Darius had also been born, raised and mostly stayed within the Seven Roads's zip code, Price had a penchant for gossip, and Rose had a way with locations. Her husband, the only local mechanic, also had proven to be an asset when it came to local information-gathering.

"He was staying at the new hotel with the rest of the wedding party and last seen this morning in the lobby. Doc

Ernest says he hasn't been dead for more than a few hours. Wherever he was killed, we need to find it."

Rose nodded.

Price looked to Darius.

"Have you talked to the brother yet? Mitchell Keys?" he asked. "I heard it's not looking that great for him."

Darius hadn't.

Which led to one of the complications the sheriff now sighed about.

Rose picked up on the tension quickly.

"What? Let me guess. He started yelling for a lawyer?"

Liam shook his head.

"No," he answered. "His fiancée."

Darius felt the same flash of annoyance as he had when Mitchell had said the same thing to him no less than half an hour beforehand.

"What?" Price asked.

"He's refusing to say anything until he can talk to his fiancée, not a lawyer, not his brother. Just Miss Myers. And he wants to talk to her privately first."

Price snorted.

"Well, that's not suspicious or anything," he said.

The sheriff nodded.

"I agree. And normally we wouldn't even entertain that idea but—" Liam looked to Darius "—Detective Williams has done something that he apparently has never done before during the span of his entire career that's made me rethink our next steps."

Three heads turned in sync.

Darius didn't think it was that big of a deal.

Yet, he straightened his back as he spoke.

"I vouched for her. I vouched for Evelyn Myers."

Chapter Six

Her phone died sometime between arriving at the sheriff's department and being told to wait in Darius's office. It was unfortunate timing. And annoying.

Darius had left the small box of a room what felt like hours ago, but Eve logically knew it was probably closer to twenty minutes she sat there alone.

Unlike the boy she had once spent all her time with, this adult version called Detective Williams seemed to be more fond of debilitating silences instead of idle chatter. Once he made it clear that he wasn't going to give her a crumb of information about Mitchell or Gary's death, he had gone quiet in the truck. It had forced Eve to play around in her own head while she waited to arrive at their destination.

That play hadn't lasted long.

She kept bumping up against two problems, and neither one of them had an easy solution.

Gary had been shot and moved to the wedding ceremony, right? That meant something. But what? And who would do it?

The other problem was Eve's whole reason for the wedding in the first place. She had thought stopping the ceremony would give her what she needed to finally, *finally* take the almighty White Knight down.

Now?

Now she was sitting in the sheriff's department, her only partner in crime holed up somewhere else within the building, most likely a nervous wreck.

Not for the first time since Darius told her to stay in his office, Eve glanced at the door.

Maybe if she slipped out and went looking for Mitchell herself, no one would notice: she wasn't wearing her wedding dress anymore. It wasn't like she was anyone of consequence when it came to the guests she had been standing in front of a few hours ago.

Eve chewed on her lip, this time really contemplating the move, when the doorknob turned under her gaze.

Darius had a folder in one hand. He used the other to point to her mouth.

"Whatever bad idea you and that poor lip you always chew on have, go ahead and park it here," he said. "Let me remind you you're at a sheriff's department and not some movie theater you can go sneaking around in."

Eve blew out her own exasperation. She decided rolling her eyes was too much, but she knew her tone let him know it was missing.

"I'm not some kid anymore. I don't need you telling me what I should or shouldn't do."

Darius snorted. He took his seat opposite her. The framed picture she had already studied at length that sat between them showed Darius in the middle of a group of people at what looked like a mechanic's shop. Some of those faces Eve recognized as the law, others seemed to be their partners and children. Darius was sandwiched between an extremely tall man and a teenaged girl with pretty blond hair.

She didn't think the girl was his daughter, and several

glances at his ring finger made her believe that Darius was single.

Or, at least, not married.

She wouldn't put it past him to leave the rest of his sentimental pictures at home. He had never been a big sharer, after all.

But, shared past or not, the present was more important than figuring out his current relationship status.

She needed to talk to Mitchell.

So she made sure he heard that need one more time.

"Can I see Mitchell now?"

Darius leaned back in his chair a little. The folder didn't leave his hand.

"Which is what your fiancé keeps saying too. Minus the seeing part. Instead, he keeps saying *talk*. 'I need to talk to Evelyn.'"

She felt a fake smile trying to hurry and hide her rising anxiousness. Darius had always been good at seeing through the few times she had put on a fake smile as kids.

Now wasn't the time to see if that skill still worked.

"There's nothing wrong with wanting to see or talk to me after something like this happened," she pointed out.

Darius was quick, but his words felt like they were lounging.

"No, not strange at all, but what has a few of us scratching our heads is who he won't let us talk to."

Eve felt her eyebrow rise.

"Who? Scott?" She shook her head a little. "You know Mitchell is his own man and doesn't constantly need his brother for everything." Eve didn't like how Darius looked so comfortable all of a sudden. To push her own point home, she contrasted his stance. She crossed her arms over her chest.

Darius's expression was impassive.

"Men with money and backing like the Keys typically call for a lawyer first."

"Gary Whittaker is the Keyses' family lawyer. You can see why he wouldn't be asking for him."

Even to her own ears Eve heard her voice go sharp.

Darius didn't budge.

"And, again, men with money and backing like the Keys can surely find themselves another lawyer when needed."

In hindsight, Eve would realize she had glossed over how the last word changed the entire situation. Mitchell needed a lawyer, not wanted one.

He *needed* one.

But Eve didn't hear the meaning in the moment. Instead, she simply doubled down.

"Maybe he needs me more. Now, can I see him or not?"

Darius was quiet a moment. Then he rapped the desktop with his knuckle twice.

"Yeah, you can, but under one condition."

"And what's that, Detective?"

Darius didn't skip a beat with his answer.

"I have to be with you."

A heaviness settled against Eve's chest. That would make talking impossible. Or maybe not. She looked into those dark eyes and wondered how much she could get past them.

Sure, they had once been inseparable, but then they had indeed gone their own ways.

Darius might have known her then. That didn't mean he knew her now.

"Only you?" she clarified.

Darius nodded.

Eve's anxiety spiked. She would also realize later that,

in that moment, she also was skimming over one very obvious fact.

She *also* wasn't being given a choice.

Eve let out a small breath. Then she agreed.

"Let's go."

THE ROOM HAD a whiteboard against the wall on one side, a long table with chairs tucked underneath it in the middle, and Mitchell Keys in a tux against the back wall.

During Darius's career he had seen all kinds of people waiting in the big room. Victims, loved ones, witnesses, colleagues and suspects he didn't want to spook with an actual interrogation room. He had walked alongside them, let them lead or sat in his usual chair, waiting for them to be brought in.

He had seen reactions from every angle.

Sadness. Anger. Happiness. Apathy. Confusion. Exhaustion.

It all blended in a carousel of memory.

So he shouldn't have been surprised at the reaction the ill-fated, almost-married couple gave when Eve walked into the room ahead of him.

And yet, Darius couldn't help but pause in the doorway.

Mitchell Keys might not have been the same as his brother, but so far he had been holding himself with a rigidness that was nearly contagious. Anxiety and a twitch beneath the skin just itching to get out. Darius had expected that anxiety to lessen at the sight of Eve because that was what he believed to be a normal reaction. To see the woman you were supposed to marry after a tragedy kept it from happening? After you clearly hadn't been able to talk anything out with each other?

Never mind being the number one suspect in a homicide investigation.

However, the second Mitchell laid eyes on Eve, there was only one emotion that was so palpable that Darius nearly felt it too.

Relief.

Undeniable and absolute relief.

So much so that the man who had once had a decent height to him, lost an inch or so as he sagged into an exhale. In one moment he was taut, a rubber band ready to snap, in the next he was melted ice cream, pooling on the old carpet floor.

And Eve's reaction to *his* reaction was just as surprising.

She didn't mirror the relief. Not one bit.

In fact, when the couple met each other in the middle of the room, the tension that had fallen from Mitchell seemed to be freezing up into Eve. Like he had passed the buck through simple eye contact. Her shoulders were straight as a board by the time she reached him.

For the third time in the span of seconds, Darius was surprised.

Instead of some kind of intimate embrace or kiss, Eve simply reached her hands out and grabbed his.

Then she patted them.

It reminded Darius of a grandparent trying to assure a child who had just been scolded by a parent. Protective and loving.

She's not in love with him.

The thought flashed into Darius's mind in the steps between the doorway to his usual chair at the table. By the time he was settled into it, he decided the unprompted suspicion was, in fact, true.

Even if Eve hadn't asked him to stop the wedding, he would have drawn the same conclusion.

However, adding in the wedding itself: the social, easy-to-talk-to Eve had had no friends standing at her side; the bridesmaids were associates and hand-me-downs from Scott Keys; her family also wasn't in the audience. No Drake Myers, a father she had loved dearly when they were kids. No aunt. No cousins. No one.

Just a room filled with fancy outfits and concern at the interruption.

But not concern for Eve.

Even now, her fiancé wasn't the one offering reassurance.

It was Eve who was comforting him.

Darius didn't know what it could possibly be, but he knew then that Eve was up to something. Given her genuine shock at Gary Whittaker's death, he didn't think a homicide was a part of whatever she was doing.

The jury on Mitchell Keys, however, was still out for Darius. It was why he and the sheriff had made sure that at least one of them would be in the room when the two reunited. Something that Mitchell didn't seem to mind at all. His gaze was glued to Eve's.

"How are you holding up?" she asked the groom. "My phone died, or else I would have already called."

Mitchell shook his head. While the sheriff had spent most of his time talking to the man, Darius had introduced himself at the library. He hadn't been verbose or charming then. Just simple.

Now there was a softness to his words. There was affection, but again, it wasn't what Darius had expected from a future husband.

"Scott was holding my phone for the ceremony, and I

didn't get a chance to grab it back before he went off with the sheriff," he explained to her. "When I tried to call from one of the phones here, they wouldn't let me."

Darius switched his gaze to Eve at that.

Her shoulders stayed tight.

"It's okay. Everything is going to be fine." Eve gave one more hand pat. Instead of pulling away after, she kept her hand right on top of Mitchell's. From her profile, Darius could see her open her mouth a little and then close it. She waited a beat, then finally chose the words she seemed to want to say. "Everything we were going to do? We're still going to get it done. This only pauses our plans, not ends them, okay?"

Darius felt his eyebrow rise.

Mitchell nodded.

His *Okay* was just as soft as before.

Darius would have expected more talk between them, but Eve turned to face him, dropping Mitchell's hands in the process. Her voice changed yet again. This time, it was a tone he recognized.

Determination.

Pure and true.

"We have things to do," she said. "So what do we need to give you before we can leave? A written statement?"

Like Darius knew that Eve wasn't in love with Mitchell Keys, he knew right then and there that Eve truly hadn't put together one and one yet. That he hadn't taken her to the department to be reunited with her fiancé or simply do paperwork.

He wasn't her childhood friend right now.

He was Detective Williams.

A part of him didn't like the feeling.

The other part domed his fingers on top of the table.

He met Eve's stare head on.

"The only way he's leaving is if he has an alibi."

Eve's eyebrows slammed together in complete confusion.

"An alibi?" she repeated. "For what?"

Darius felt the weight of his badge against his chest. His answer was as clear as could be.

"For the murder of Gary Whittaker."

Chapter Seven

She wasn't a small woman, but she wasn't big either. Eve was average. Compared to Darius? Maybe that average lost a few inches. Physically, at least. She had to tilt her chin up to meet his eye but didn't need to put too much space between them to get a good angle to do it.

She jogged for exercise when she had the time and was toned in some places, squishier in others. The muscles Darius had built since he was a kid had even the toughest of hers beat three to zero.

He had the law hanging around his neck in a badge. Eve had Scott Keys's personal passwords memorized.

The differences in their divide were easy to see. Where one shone, the other flickered; where one ran, the other stood. And in the years since they had last seen each other, Eve felt like she had been the one who had stood the most still.

Yet height, muscles, past, present, badge or not, Eve felt confident that there was one area that little kid Eve still reigned supreme over Darius.

She had a mouth on her.

A Southern one, to boot.

And an angry Southern mouth? It yelled faster than it thought and sounded off with a syrup that could choke you if you weren't prepared.

Eve couldn't tell now if Darius had expected it, but she knew Mitchell hadn't. The moment her volume rose above her average height, she felt one of his hands at the back of her elbow.

It did nothing to calm her.

"And here I thought you were just trying to be nice to an old friend, but it turns out you were just buttering me up to lob an absolutely ridiculous accusation at my fiancé *on our wedding day*," Eve started in. "No wonder you were waiting for me at the library and offering me rides! Also, I track you down to ask you for help, and now I'm having to defend myself not even a few hours later? The absolute gall of you, Darius Fitzgerald Williams!"

Mitchell did a little squeeze against her skin.

Darius simply sighed out.

"I never buttered you up or lobbed anything at you, and I'm not being ridiculous," he said. "In fact, as you just said yourself, you were the one who came to find me. Not the other way around."

He left out the part where the reason she had come looking for him in the first place was to ask to *stop* the wedding she had just become defensive about. If Eve hadn't been so hot under the collar, she would have thought nice on the kindness of not pointing that out in mixed company.

Darius leaned forward a little and kept on before she could get rolling again.

"I'm asking a question about a current homicide case." Darius pointed over her shoulder but kept her stare. "And, if I say so myself, I'm being pretty polite about doing it here first and not throwing both of you into an uncomfortable interrogation room to do it. So, if you would stop using my full name like I owe you money and take a breath and a seat, we can get this all moving somewhere other than right into a fight. Does that sound good to you, Evelyn Rebecca Myers?"

Eve's nostrils flared. Her face scrunched. Both acts were like stretching before really starting to run. If she had been twelve, she would have kept going, louder than sin, but Eve the adult had picked up a little decorum in the last decade or so.

She also was starting to remember where she was and who was behind her.

If she had been solo in the same situation, she would have summoned more spitfire.

But she wasn't by herself.

Mitchell needed her, and no murder accusation was going to make her stop protecting him.

"You don't owe me money, you owe me *you*," Eve finally muttered, pulling back the chair closest to her. Darius didn't react to talk of their childhood promise and only watched as she settled across from him. He waited for Mitchell to do the same. Then he split his attention between both.

"While we haven't found the location where Mr. Whittaker was killed, we've been able to get his time of death down to earlier today, somewhere between noon and two o'clock," he started. "Since he was obviously moved to the location of the ceremony, it's hard to ignore the theory that it was a premeditated event and not a crime of passion or one of opportunity. Which is why we looked at the wedding party for any information that might point us in a solid direction to start."

There was something to be said about dark eyes locking in on a target. Eve suppressed a little shiver as Darius moved his attention to Mitchell.

"And several fingers pointed your way, Mr. Keys," he said. "So now that Miss Myers is by your side, let me ask where you were today between the hours of twelve and two."

Mitchell had never been good at hiding his emotions; he was especially bad at hiding his anxiety. Eve knew the moment the question finished that he was already stressed about his answer. His body language, the hesitation in answering…

She also knew before he said a word that he was going to lie.

"I was in my hotel room. With Eve."

The lie was short. Its aftereffects were going to ripple far.

"You were in your hotel room," Darius repeated, tone impassive. "With Eve."

Mitchell nodded.

"I-I'm not big into crowds like my brother is. I was nervous and needed someone to help me calm down."

"So you asked to see the bride before the wedding. That's bad luck, you know."

Mitchell nodded again. The movement was stiff.

"I know, but seeing her always makes me feel better."

Like the lie, this truth was also short, but Eve knew it was genuine. She would have felt the warmth from it, had a coldness not started to spread throughout her body.

The fact of the matter was she hadn't been with Mitchell from noon until two. She hadn't seen him in person until she had been walking down the aisle toward him.

But could Darius prove that? Was there evidence he already had that Mitchell was lying? Had someone seen him or her out and about without the other during that time?

Instead of immediately agreeing, Eve tried to steer the conversation in a different direction.

"Mitchell had over two hundred people who can put him at the altar around the time when Gary was moved to the lobby," she pointed out. "He couldn't have done that. At least one of us would have noticed if he had stepped out mid vows."

Darius was quick.

"Just because he didn't move the body doesn't mean he didn't have anything to do with Mr. Whittaker's death."

"So you're saying you think he killed Gary and then—what?" she said. "Then, he had someone place poor Gary in the lobby after the ceremony started? Why? That makes no sense."

"I'm not saying anything at the moment," Darius shot back. "I was *asking* where Mr. Keys here was during the hours between twelve and two today. And now I'm asking *you* the same question."

Darius's expression remained impassive. His tone, however, had hardened.

Eve matched his energy.

"Mitchell already answered that," she replied.

"But you didn't." Darius leaned forward, those dark eyes on a new target. "So let me be clear in what I'm asking now so you can be just as clear with your answer. Where were you, Eve, during the hours of twelve and two today?"

Eve could picture the house in front of her. She could feel the grass under her bare feet. She could smell smoke coming from somewhere in the neighborhood, probably someone grilling in their backyard. She remembered shivering at the cold but not as bad as she would later, since she hadn't yet changed into her wedding dress yet.

Her childhood home.

That's where she had been earlier that day, still undecided about what to do next to get out of the wedding. To stop from being legally tied to the Keyses. To instead use the change in their crumbling plan to her and Mitchell's advantage.

She had just been staring and thinking about the present and future. Then, without realizing it, nostalgia from the past had swept her worries away for a while. Only a glance at her watch later had pulled her from her quiet recollection.

Whatever plan she would make would have to come after she donned her wedding dress.

So at 1:42 p.m., she had left the front lawn of her childhood home and hurried over to the bridal party's dressing room at the old library to get ready. No thoughts of using Darius had crept in until she had taken off her engagement ring and caught sight of the scar on her hand.

Before that?

She hadn't seen or talked to Mitchell at all during those two hours.

It was one thing to not correct Darius about Mitchell's lie.

It was another to lie directly to his face.

But Eve wasn't back in town to reminisce about the boy she had once promised to take care of for the rest of their lives. She was there to stop a man filled with greed, malice and power.

Eve took in a deep breath. She released it as she spoke clearly.

"I was with Mitchell Keys in his hotel room."

And, just like that, Eve lied to become a murder suspect's alibi.

However, the worst part?

She knew that Darius knew it too.

HE WASN'T ONE to pitch a fit but there he was—pitching it.

Darius threw his bag down against the couch. Like the rest of the furniture in his house, it wasn't new, but it definitely wasn't worn either. He rarely spent time lounging around, and that went double for lounging around in his home. If there was any one spot in all of Seven Roads that was worn because of him, it was his desk chair at the office or the strip of carpet that ran in front of his desk at home.

He was a man who was used to living in his work, pacing in his home, and only using his off time to do the necessities in life.

It was how he had been living between the walls of his childhood home since he had been the last one left.

Pitching a fit? Throwing a tantrum? Being annoyed enough to throw his bag and then start cussing?

That was the part of his work and life routine that was abnormal.

As was the fact of someone already inside of the house, answering back.

Theo Weaver hurried into the living room with a frying pan in one hand, a cell phone in the other and an expression that looked split between caution and fear. Add in the fact that he was wearing the joke apron his dad had bought Darius a few years back that read *Don't kiss the chef, I have trust issues* and the sight might have been comical enough to force Darius to see the humor in it.

Instead, he grumbled deep.

It was the first time since Theo had moved into his guest bedroom after his graduation that Darius had legitimately forgotten that he now had a temporary roommate.

One who was, unfortunately, very smart.

Trying to avoid the obvious wouldn't work here.

Theo's wide eyes lost their worry. He lowered his phone but kept the frying pan level.

"Are we good?" he asked in greeting. Theo eyed the bag

Darius had just thrown. Darius ran a hand through his hair and took a beat to crack his neck to the side.

"Sorry," he said. "It's been a day."

Darius belatedly looked around for signs of another bag or purse. Theo caught the sweep.

"Winnie already left," he said. "She said she couldn't concentrate on her interviews after everything that's been going on." He smirked. "Between you and me, I think she just wanted to go gab with her dad and JJ about the whole wedding drama."

Darius suppressed another grumble and followed Theo into the kitchen.

"Winnie doesn't like gossiping," he reminded the boy. "It's one of the better traits of yours that you share with her. You two only give what you need to, and even then, it's like an act of God to get information out of you. I can't imagine if you two ever made another human together."

Theo made a noise of disgust.

Darius didn't think it was genuine, but he let his joke lie.

A bowl filled with scrambled eggs, sausage and other little things was on the counter. Darius was surprised to see a second one next to it.

"Winnie told me to make you whatever I was having for dinner and put it in the fridge just in case, but I guess your timing worked out," Theo explained. "Though, honestly, I thought you wouldn't leave the department at all tonight."

Darius felt some of the anger in him release a little. He gave the boy a pat on the shoulder and a quick thanks. He made a mental note to return the favor to Winnie sometime soon. For all their fights and youthful annoyances, there was no denying these kids were thoughtful.

They settled into the small dining nook and ate their breakfast-for-dinner bowls in silence. Darius might have vented a little, but his shoulders lined with a tension that seemed to seep downward and spread. It was only after Theo placed his fork into his empty bowl that Theo addressed it.

"I'm guessing the Mitchell Keys lead didn't pan out," he said, as neutral as the sheriff when he was being matter-of-fact. Darius glared. Theo raised his hands in self-defense. "Winnie and I might be stars in the tight-lipped department but that can't be said for a good majority of McCoy County's finest. Try as everyone might, some information slips out."

Darius knew that no matter how hard he tried to keep a lid on the investigation Theo was right. Details and information would get out.

That's why he hadn't yelled at Eve right then and there in the meeting room.

You're lying, he'd wanted to shout.

But, for one, he had never yelled at Eve a day in his life, and he wanted to take that achievement to the grave. And, for two, if anyone found out that Eve was lying about an alibi—an alibi in a murder investigation, to boot?

Darius shook his head now even at the thought.

It would get out. It would put suspicion on her. It could ruin her.

But what if she is involved? What if she's covering for Mitchell?

These two thoughts had been on repeat since he'd had to let the couple leave. Darius hadn't for a moment thought Eve had killed Gary or had a hand in his death, but would she really cover for Mitchell if *he* had?

It was a question that grated against Darius.

Maybe he had been wrong about her relationship with the younger Keys brother. Maybe she was in love with him. She was, he believed, lying to law enforcement for him. That wasn't some typical friendly thing to do, was it?

Theo was still looking at him.

Darius sighed out and let his fork clink into the bowl beneath his hands.

"Everyone in the wedding party alibied out," he skirted. "Almost all the guests came into town right before the wedding. There were only six who could have been here during the kill window. And, of those six, none had connections to Mr. Whittaker."

"And no one knows where he was actually killed yet," Theo added. Again, he raised his hands in defense. This time he added a smirk. "You can blame me hearing that from the sheriff himself. He pulled me and Blake into a video call to ask us career locals about places around here y'all might have not thought about."

If it had been anyone else other than Blake, Liam's wife, Theo's adoptive mother, and one of the fiercest former sheriffs he had ever known, Darius might have taken offense at asking outside of the department for help. Instead, he knew to be grateful she had taken time out of her own job to try and give them more than they had.

Which was still almost nothing, if Darius were being honest.

"I'm assuming, since I haven't been called in, that nothing came from that conversation?" he asked.

Theo made a gun with his hand.

"Bingo. Blake couldn't think of anything y'all had missed, and now that she's been back in town for years, she's more of an expert on this town than me."

Darius rubbed at his neck. Sighing wasn't going to do a thing, but he felt the urge again.

So there was a strong possibility that it happened outside of Seven Roads, making an already-difficult search even more so.

"This is one of those few times I wish a victim had been more into social media," Darius said after a moment. "Mr. Whittaker's last few days have been hard to pin down. We can't even confirm yet when he first got into town. He's not married or in a relationship either, so there's no one who seems to have had a good itinerary for him leading up to the wedding. Usually social media can help us with things like that."

For the next few minutes, they went back and forth with questions and answers that Darius had, for the most part, already gone over back at the department. No new insights sprang up, and no missing information shook loose.

Darius's patience, however, dissolved into a tiredness that he decided not to ignore any longer. He warned Theo not to stay up too late, washed his dishes and only paused in the kitchen doorway as an afterthought.

"You and Winnie never asked about it, but I want to explain."

Theo turned his way, bowl in one hand, dish soap in the other. His eyebrow rose. Darius, so sure in every word he spoke about work, felt an uncomfortableness ease into an explanation he hadn't originally intended to give.

"Evelyn Myers used to live in the house next door," he started, motioning to the house outside to the right. "We were friends as kids until her dad got a job up north and they moved. Today was the first day I'd seen her since then."

"And she thought you two were still close enough to ask you to stop her wedding?"

It was a fair question for anyone to ask, and Darius couldn't fault the boy for his bluntness.

In return, he gave a simple answer.

"I'm not sure why she wanted the wedding stopped, but I owed her a favor, so I was going to do it."

"That's a big favor to ask," Theo said. "She must have really done something big for it to hold water all these years."

Again, Darius stuck to a truth that was as honest as they came.

He nodded.

"She saved my life."

He didn't explain further, and Theo didn't pry past that. Darius moved down the same hallway he'd walked since he had learned how to walk but paused at the door on the right. It was Theo's room now: years ago it had been his.

Part of Darius was glad to have moved to the main bedroom at the end of the hall—it was bigger, he'd updated it, and there was an attached private bathroom that was nice too—but sometimes when his mind went to the past, he missed the one thing that his new room didn't have.

The view from its window had been one of a kind.

This time, Darius did sigh.

It came out low and long enough to carry him back to the present.

That night he fell asleep quickly.

In the morning, he was up before his alarm went off at seven.

Despite forgetting to turn the heat on, he was surprisingly warm.

Then that warmth moved.

Someone was next to him in bed.

Darius's eyes were open in a flash. Adrenaline exploded in his veins, and every muscle he had seemed ready to spring into action. It was only by the grace of God that he recognized who it was pressed against his side before his fight instincts fully kicked in.

The person in question was unbothered by the internal struggle.

Then again, Evelyn Myers had always been a heavy sleeper.

Chapter Eight

Raina Myers was a nice, fair woman. She wasn't unkind or abusive, didn't cuss or yell. Paid full price, donated to charity, and always drove the speed limit. Her grades had been good, her friends happy, and even though her parents had died young, she had been old enough to cherish them. Most everyone who knew Raina even believed that the love she'd shared with her parents would transfer to her future children after she had married.

So it took longer than it would have otherwise for most to admit—in hushed waves of gossip—that those people were wrong. Raina might have been a nice, fair woman, but when it came to being a mother, she'd decided she didn't have time for it.

That's why the smallest Myers was still outside long after the sun had gone down the first time she met Darius Williams.

The then-seven-year-old had been trying to run away and had been horrible at it. Something that the six-year-old Eve had had to point out.

"You'll hurt your leg if you do it that way."

Her voice had been small but easy to hear in the side yard between their houses. She had a bat in one hand while the other should have held a softball had she not lost it. She had decided to play golf with the two and had realized quickly that the porch lights and streetlamp in the distance weren't doing the best to illuminate her makeshift golf course.

It had been quite the shock to see the neighbor's window slide open and a boy around her age start trying to climb out.

He, on the other hand, seemed to be much more shocked. Once her voice broke through the quiet of the night air, his backward climb out of the window turned into more of a downward spiral. It wasn't that far of a drop, but the angle was all wrong, and Eve knew all too well that it was the angles that got you most of the time. She'd once jumped from the back of a pickup truck with ease but had misstepped on the porch stairs and landed wrong enough to twist her ankle.

She'd cried for a long time after that.

Now she knew to watch for angles.

The boy was going to hurt himself if he fell the way he was going, so Eve dropped her bat and closed the space between them just in time to become a pillow.

She tried to stop his fall but instead met him as he fell backward. They hit the grass with a little more than a thud. Eve had her arms wrapped around from his back to his chest and kept her hold a few moments after everything had stilled.

He wasn't heavy enough to knock the breath out of her, but the book bag that he had thrown out of the window before his scurry down looked like it would have done the trick had he been wearing it.

Eve glanced at it as the boy rolled off her to the side and sprang up to his feet. His eyes were wide and dark as they were finally about to take her in.

"You—you're the girl—" he pointed to her house "—you're the neighbor."

Eve laughed and stood, dusting off her jeans.

She pointed to the window opposite the one he had just fallen from.

"Eve Myers. That's my room." She gave him a questioning look. "Who are you? I haven't seen you before."

The couple who had moved into the house next door had done so while Eve had been at school. Or maybe when she was out at the park. Maybe it had been when she was trying to sneak onto the Becker farmland that wasn't too far from where they were now.

Either way, she hadn't known the new owners had any kids.

Suddenly, she found herself extremely excited at the prospect.

The boy was shy in his nod.

He rubbed at his arm.

"I start school next week. My name's Darius."

The rising excitement was too much for the small Eve. She dropped her bat and jumped up and down in place.

"*Finally*, I can have someone to play with," she exclaimed. "I get so bored here by myself! What are you doing now? Do you want to play golf?"

She scooped the bat back up and held it out like a queen presenting a knight with his sword.

"I'll let you go first," she added. "We just have to find the ball. I was hitting it in the front yard, but it rolled to the street, and I think I hit it a little too hard to get it back, and it *sounded* like it might have hit that gutter…"

Eve rattled off all the possible trajectories she believed her ratty softball had gone, half expecting him to stop her and half expecting him to ignore her if she managed to finish her train of thought.

However, the boy who had just fallen out of the window

turned those wide eyes and their dark gaze around to the unexplored space between the houses. Eve followed him as he walked over to the tall parts of the grass toward the back corners and bent over slightly.

By the time she realized he was searching for the ball, he had found it.

Darius presented the surrogate golf ball to Eve without comment.

Eve was grinning ear to ear as she took it.

"This is going to be so much fun!"

The next few minutes she explained her rules, gave Darius some tips and challenged the boy to a new game. And that's what they did for next hour or so. Chatted and played. Eve didn't ask why he had been trying to leave, and Darius didn't ask why no one seemed to notice that Eve had already been gone.

It was only when Eve yawned out big that she decided her bed was calling her name.

"Do you need me to help you climb back in?" Darius asked, pointing to her bedroom window.

Eve shook her head.

"I can just go through the front door," she said. "No one will notice."

Eve nodded to the window across from hers.

"Want me to help you climb?"

Darius seemed tall enough to be able to do it himself now that he wasn't going backward.

"I can pull myself back in," he said.

Eve was so excited that the boy had chosen not to complete his plan of running away that she threw her arms around him in a quick hug. He stiffened in her embrace and still looked uncomfortable after she let go.

But Eve didn't care. She finally had someone to talk to.

She tossed the bat and ball into the grass and pointed once again to her window.

"I'll open my curtain when I get inside so you can see me!"

And that's just what she did. After running through her house, slowing slightly at her mother's door, and then bounding into her bedroom, Eve flung open her bedroom curtain and looked out.

Darius sure was impressive. He was already back inside his room. His window was still open. Eve was impatient as she opened hers too.

"Do you want to play tomorrow?" she asked, trying not to be too loud.

"I'm grounded for the weekend," he called back. "I can't leave the house."

Nothing was going to—or could—stop the excitement that Darius's sudden existence had unlocked in her. Not even his parents.

"Don't worry," Eve yell-whispered. "I'll come to you."

The next night that's exactly what she did. When his parents went to their bedroom, Darius unlocked his window to find a green-eyed girl staring up at him. He pulled her and the bag of toys up the wall and over the windowsill with relative ease.

After that, it became a routine. Darius kept his window unlocked, and whether it was daytime or not, there was always an Eve who eventually crawled on through. Sometimes they would play, sometimes they would just talk. As they got older, the foot of his bed became their dedicated homework-and-study spot. When things at their respective homes became difficult, the time spent in his room became longer.

Then, one night, Eve hadn't left.

A storm had made her empty house seem terrifying for once, and Darius had done what he did best and knew what she needed without asking. He'd given her his bed and made a pallet for himself on the floor next to it. Eve had fallen asleep to the sound of his voice while the storm raged on outside.

That was how Eve realized there was only one thing in her life that was certain, and that one thing was Darius Williams.

HER HAIR WAS WILD, thrown across his pillow and arm like an escapee finally sensing freedom. Her clothes were a little more restrained. She was wearing jeans, a black tank top and socks with rainbows printed on them. Darius only knew this because the side of her that wasn't touching him was partially uncovered.

Eve was a kicker in her sleep.

But he only knew that from having seen her thrash around from a safe spot on his floor when they were kids.

He'd never experienced it in his bed.

With him in it.

Eve's little movements turned into a big stretch and yawn. Darius, unsure of exactly what to do, waited until her eyelids slowly opened.

She blinked a few times before angling her head to the side to look up at him.

When the green met his dark, he reacted instinctually.

"What the hell, Eve!"

Like some shy teenage boy, he bolted upright. The sheet and blanket slid down his bare upper body. He clutched at them, pulling then back up. The memory of him silently trying to decide what top to wear after his shower the night before—and ultimately deciding not to wear anything at all—flashed through his mind.

Thank goodness he'd opted for bottoms, at the very least.

Eve also sat up but with way less effort and concern. She rubbed at her hair and then motioned to the closed bedroom door.

"What the hell right back at you, Darius," she said. "I almost climbed into the wrong dang room with another whole man in it! Since when did you change rooms?"

Darius couldn't believe what he was hearing.

"Since I bought the house after Dad moved to Montana— Wait. You tried to get into Theo's room? Did he see you?"

Eve was fast with that. "No! Once I realized the window was locked, I finally really looked through the gap in the curtain and realized he was too young to be your grumpy butt. Who is he?" For the first time since waking up, she finally showed some form of panic. "Wait. Is he *your kid*? You're not married! I checked!"

Her voice had gone high. On reflex Darius slapped a hand over her mouth.

"Stop crowing so loud, woman," he hissed. "And no, not married, and no, not my kid. He's Sheriff Weaver's boy."

Darius had enough muscle memory in him to know that he better let go quick before she bit him, so he dropped his hand with a warning look thrown her way for good measure.

To her credit, she adjusted her volume.

"The sheriff's son? Why are you living with the sheriff's son? Is the sheriff the one who moved in next door?"

Darius held up his hand in a *Stop* gesture.

"Theo just graduated college and is interning," he explained. "He has a lot of young siblings at home and wanted a little more quiet when he came back to town. I offered my spare room until he could save a little more money for his own place. And no, the sheriff isn't the one who bought the house next door."

Eve flopped back in the bed like she owned it.

"Well, if there's one thing you're good at, it's being quiet," she said. "Playing hide-and-seek with you as kids was harder than any waitressing job I've had since."

"That's only because when it was your turn to hide, you couldn't stop giggling," he pointed out. "I didn't need to be good at hide-and-seek. I just needed to wait for you to give up because you were bored."

She tapped her feet together and didn't disagree.

Then Darius came back to his senses.

He turned to face her completely. The top sheet and cover fell again at the movement. This time he didn't bother with them.

"Eve," he said, voice stern, "why are you here? In my house. *In my bed?*"

She sat up in a flash, clearly offended.

"What?" She pointed to the floor beside the bed. "Did you expect me to sleep on the floor like when we were kids? Not to point out the obvious, but this bed is gigantic compared to your old bed. There's plenty of room for like three of me to fit here." She swept her hand over her lap and toward him to, he assumed, show all the space there was around them. However, there were two problems with that.

One, there was no space between them. Or, at least, there hadn't been when they'd first woken up. Two, her hand paused in midair. Her gaze did not.

It was as obvious as the moon in the night sky that Eve had just put together the fact that Darius wasn't wearing anything above the waist.

"Wow. I guess you turned into one of those guys who exercises, huh? Look at all these muscles. And here I thought I was in good-enough shape."

She reached out her hand, and he knew with every bone in his body that her intention was to feel said muscles. Because she was Eve and he was Darius and, a long time ago, they were Eve and Darius. She was comfortable with him; he'd built a door in the wall that always was around him for her.

Being this close was nothing for them.

Yet, just as he could see the old scar along the side of her hand, Darius could see the engagement ring on her finger.

Both were quick reminders that time had indeed separated them.

Darius caught her hand before she could make contact with his chest.

When he spoke, his words had a warning carefully carved into the tone.

"Eve, tell me right now why you're here."

Her hand was warm in his.

The rest of her went tense.

With one look, Darius knew she had finally come around to being serious. Talk of their past, of their friendship, of the years between then and now all went to the back burner.

Eve sighed out sharply.

Her words came out steady.

"I think I know who killed Gary Whittaker."

Darius's eyebrows rose.

"Who?"

Eve didn't flinch.

"Me," she said. "I think it was me."

Chapter Nine

He was still mad. Big mad. Mad enough that even sitting in the cab of his truck half an hour after her admission, Darius was still giving her the cold shoulder.

And Eve couldn't take it anymore.

"I said I was sorry," she tried. "I'm big enough to admit that maybe I crossed a line by coming to you with this now."

Darius snorted.

"You mean breaking and entering into my house and bed and then casually telling me you've been lying about a homicide case? Eve, you couldn't even turn around and see the line you've crossed, because it's so far back."

He turned off the engine and slid the key into his front pocket.

"The window was unlocked so it was entering, not breaking. And I lied to you about Gary because I didn't even think about it until last night when I was in bed. So it wasn't really a lie. It was just a connection that I hadn't made yet." She held up her finger. "Though, I have to remind you, as soon as I made it, I came over to you."

"And instead of waking me up, you got under my sheets."

The memory of the bare-chested Darius popped into Eve's head so quick that she stumbled in her response.

"I—Well—I—" She took a breath. Her cheeks grew warm.

Darius was a looker, no contest, but she hadn't expected looking *at* him like that would do as much as it had done to her. Eve fought the urge to try and wipe the blush that was no doubt turning her cheeks as red as a Stop sign and powered through her defense. "I figured it was better to let you sleep since this didn't seem like a problem that would get worse with a few hours. Plus, if I'm being honest, I haven't been getting the best sleep over the last month or so, and your bed is a memory foam. It would have been harder to stay awake."

An expression she couldn't read flashed across his face before Darius turned to look out the windshield. In all of Seven Roads this was probably the one spot he hadn't expected her to direct them toward.

To be fair, it had been a surprise to Eve too when she had thought about it.

"You said you think you got Gary Whittaker killed here?"

The former Grayton Steel Mill, now owned by a company called Bellview Tech, stood sentry at the edge of Seven Roads as it had since the town's inception. The small town could survive the earth cracking in two beneath them, but they couldn't make it a week if the steel mill ever went out of business. Even Eve knew this, despite being away for years.

As the employer for most of Seven Roads, it would probably outlast all of them, their children and their children.

It was one reason why she knew Darius was so hesitant to believe that Gary Whittaker had been killed inside the back quarter of the mill's residence hall. Gary wasn't a local. He would have had no reason to be at the steel mill, never mind the residence hall.

"Most of the dorms are empty, minus a few night workers and the weekend crews who come in twice a month," he added before she could answer. "There's no reason Gary should have been here."

The residence halls were in two long buildings wrapped in brick abutting the edge of one of the steel mill's wire fences. They were parked at the side of the dirt road that led in from the main one. It looked as unused as the buildings themselves.

Eve squared her jaw.

"Because I told someone once this is the last place even a local would go for trouble."

"Someone? Do you mean Mitchell?"

Eve opened the truck door. All humor and teasing she'd had in her for the man behind the wheel was gone. The blush at her cheeks had already cooled before the cold outside met her.

"If I'm right, I'll explain everything," she said skirting his retort. "Until then, can you trust me?"

She formed it as a question but didn't wait for an answer. Eve shut the door before he could respond. She was crossing the line again, she was sure. A detective was asking her valid and reasonable questions.

And she was telling him all hands inside the cart until the ride has come to a complete stop.

Even if he hadn't been the law, it was asking a lot given the situation.

What could she do but go forward?

Darius, at least, didn't fight her on it. He walked around the hood of the truck and fixed his belt. In between Eve sneaking back out of his window and across the side yard to his truck and him leaving the house, he had put himself into a good pair of jeans and a gray-and-black bomber jacket. Along with his height, it created a look of casual but potent intimidation.

That went double when his voice ground out low.

"Let's go, then."

The gate wasn't anything to speak of, and the same went for any security cameras or guards in the area. Darius commented on it as he nudged the gate open with his shoulder and motioned her through.

"Theo used to work here part-time in the cafeteria and said the new management cares as much as the old crew about keeping the back quarter guarded."

"So they don't care at all either."

He nodded.

"No reason to waste money watching nothing," he said. "Honestly, I'm surprised they haven't shut this entire section down. Or at least demolished it to build something else here. The new company that took it over seems to have more than enough funds to do it."

So she had been right after all. Her off-the-cuff story about the residence halls had stayed true even after she had left town.

"Dad used to hate staying in them during his long shifts," she said. "He said he imagined it was like being in a college dorm, but instead of a bunch of guys goofing around and having fun in their gym shorts, the men's residence hall was filled with grouchy men in sweaty coveralls. And they always stole his lunch out of the fridge."

Darius slowed as they approached the first pathway leading to the women's residence hall to their right. She quieted. Other than their footsteps, there were no other sounds.

The one-story building was an eerie setting against the cold silence.

She waited for Darius to make a silent decision. Once he kept moving to the path that led to the men's residence hall to the left, she followed.

Her stomach started to twist as they got closer. Her nerves sharpened. Eve almost jumped when Darius spoke low again.

"How is your dad doing?" he asked. "I didn't see him at the wedding."

Eve had been asked countless times over the last few months why her father wasn't attending the wedding. Why her family wasn't there. If she realized how sad that would look in pictures. In the press.

Or how lucky she was to have no one there but Scott Keys and his family and associates.

She had had the same stock responses ready to go until they had become a reflex instead of a response.

It's why the lie almost came out first.

Eve ran her thumb across the scar on her hand and pulled the truth out instead. At least, the truth about why he wasn't there.

"He didn't know about it, actually. The wedding, I mean." Darius's wide eyes swung her way at that. "That sounds bad, but it's not that big of a deal. He's met Mitchell and knows we're engaged but never has been a fan of these flashy kinds of events. So I decided not to bother him with it."

"Not to bother your dad with your wedding?"

Eve winced at the guilt that came from hearing that come right back to her.

"There's layers to the situation," she tried.

Darius's eyebrow went sky-high.

"Layers," he deadpanned.

She nodded.

"Yeah. You know every relationship is different with their own layers. Their own issues or complications. That's me and Mitchell. No need to pull in my dad for something like this."

They walked up the steps of the men's residence hall,

but he stopped at the door. Eve thought he was about to do some nifty law-enforcement move before entering a potential crime scene. Instead, he turned to face her head on.

"Complications like you and Mitchell not actually being a real couple."

The lie never had a chance to form.

The truth was already in between them before Eve could clock it.

"Yeah."

Darius didn't flinch.

She opened her mouth to take it back, to try to cover it up—to do something—but all Eve could do was stare.

A different kind of blush crawled up her neck. Embarrassment.

She wanted to ask how he had figured it out so quickly, and she knew there was no way to convince him otherwise now, when something finally cut through the silence around them.

A car door shut in the distance behind them.

They both turned toward the direction of the gate. From where they were standing they couldn't see the gate itself, never mind what car had pulled up.

Darius's hand went to the inside of his jacket.

"Are you expecting anyone out here?" he asked.

Eve shook her head.

"I wasn't even expecting us to be out here until late last night."

She heard a button click as his hand moved within the jacket's folds.

"And no one knows you're out here?" Darius added. "What about Mitchell? You said you told him about this place once."

She shook her head again. The sound of metal moving

rattled from the direction they were staring. Someone had gone through the gate.

"No one knows I'm out here," she said, dropping her voice to a whisper. Darius had turned, and with the movement he pulled his service weapon from his shoulder holster. He kept it down as she grabbed at the elbow of his other arm.

Eve realized a few beats too late what he had said.

The need to correct him rose with an anxiousness that made her stomach grow cold.

"And it was Scott I told about this place by accident, not Mitchell."

Footsteps could be heard crunching over some of the leaves that had been brave and quick enough to fall and change with the burst of cold weather. Soon whoever was coming would be in their field of vision.

However, Darius turned to her so fast that Eve nearly yelled in surprise.

When he spoke, his voice was so deep that the rumble felt like it went right through the fabric of his jacket and into the cold of her fingers.

"You're after Scott, not Mitchell."

Another truth, though there were some nuances missing. Now she could hear the footfalls. Still, it felt important to correct him once more.

"We're both after him," she clarified. "It's the only way we can take him down."

"Why?"

Relief flooded out with Eve's next truth. Finally, she could tell someone else.

"Because all Scott Keys is is a monster in a suit."

Darius's eyes didn't widen. He didn't look shocked or mad or concerned. He didn't look like the boy next door, and he didn't look like the only detective in town.

He was just a man standing in front of a woman, look-ing as calm as could be wrapped up in a jacket and denim.

So before the gunshot went through them both, Eve couldn't help but feel a sense of contentedness.

No matter why she was back in Seven Roads, it just felt nice to be standing on a front porch with a good man like Darius Williams.

HE KILLED THE man behind Eve in the time it took to blink. The hunting rifle in his hands hit the ground as his head tipped backward.

Darius didn't have time to watch the unknown man's body fall.

There was still the person approaching from the gate.

Darius used his free arm to swoop behind Eve to keep her upright and spun around enough to get his own gun aimed and ready.

The person who had been so noisy was already there with her own gun raised high. Darius's body acted on an instinct that was much faster than any bullet would be. He threw himself and Eve back into the residence hall door with enough power that the old wood splintered at the bolt.

A gunshot cut through the air as the door gave way.

Where he should have had the time to find his balance, and Eve along with him, the world just kept turning.

He felt the floor beneath his feet crack no more than a few steps into the room. A yellow caution sticker on part of the broken door caught the corner of his eye. All Darius could do was hold Eve tight as the floor gave way.

And what he thought would be a quick fall into some kind of crawl space turned into a long plummet into darkness.

Chapter Ten

Eve ran through the hallway, one hand pressed hard on her shoulder, and the other holding a gun. Darius labored behind, his wheezing becoming more pronounced the farther they went into whatever maze they had fallen into. She wanted to stop, to check all his injuries, but there wasn't any time.

Whoever the second shooter was might have followed them. Though, their way down into the underground corridor had been less than ideal.

Eve had still been processing the fact that she had been shot when the two of them had collided against debris and concrete. Or, really, Darius had. He'd taken the brunt of the impact beneath him.

It's why she was the one holding the gun.

"My—my hand isn't working," were his first words once they both realized they were still relatively in one piece.

Their only stroke of good luck had been the sliver of light that had shown the hallway they were now currently stumbling through. Darius must have also spotted it. They pulled themselves up together, only pausing long enough for Eve to pick up the gun.

Now she was heading in the direction of the female residence hall, sure that they had stumbled into an old storage system or water-pump holding corridor that had long since been boarded-up.

That was, until she almost hit a wall.

"Hold on," she breathed out. Eve felt Darius's body heat against her back. She used the arm holding his gun to rub it against the stone in front of her. "This is a dead end? We need a light."

"My phone is in my pocket." Darius kept his voice low too, but the sturdiness in it had crumbled. He was in pain. *Pain* pain. "G-get it for me."

Wherever they were was quiet enough that the simple action of placing the gun at her feet and feeling for his phone were as loud as yelling.

Which was good because that meant they should be able to hear their pursuer if they came their way.

Eve managed to pull the phone from his pocket with one hand, careful to keep her other pressing against the wound on her shoulder. Her hand was soaked, and she knew it would hurt like hell once her adrenaline started to ebb.

But now wasn't the time to mentally hover.

Instead, she felt a wave of gratefulness at the fact that Darius had the same model phone as her. Eve had the flashlight function on and working within seconds.

Darius was smart to shy away from its beam.

From the quick flash she was still able to see a lot of blood.

"There's...there's two ways to go," Darius breathed out.

Eve and her pounding heart turned to give the discovery more light. They had, in fact, run into a dead end whereupon you had to turn left or right.

"Where *are* we?" she asked herself.

The light showed a path to the right that was almost identical to the one to the left. No sign of life either way. Both dark and seemingly endless. The path to the right had a few wooden-looking crates stacked on one side. The other to the left looked like it sloped slightly downward.

Eve motioned to the left.

"This would go toward the main part of the mill? The other way would be toward the woods? I don't... I don't know where we are."

Darius's body heat intensified as it pressed into her back. The sudden weight made her stumble into the stone wall.

"Sorry, I—" Darius was close enough that her hair moved at his words, but he couldn't have sounded farther away.

"Darius? What's wrong?"

His head dropped to the top of her good shoulder, weighing it down enough that she had trouble turning to face him. Eve wasn't able to get the light directly on his face, but she saw enough to know asking what was wrong had been a silly question.

Everything was wrong.

He was in undeniable pain.

And that pain had a terrifying consequence.

"I-I'm not dying, but I am…going to pass out," he managed. With each word she felt him become heavier. Eve let go of her shoulder to try and help somehow, but Darius's remaining bit of strength went to him pushing her hand right on back.

"Keep pressure on it." He slid off her and hit the ground before Eve could stop him.

"Darius? Darius!"

In the dim light Eve saw his eyes close. They didn't open again.

Panic as pure and solid as the ground beneath her feet grabbed ahold of Eve as she grabbed ahold of Darius. There wasn't much she could do other than keep him from falling over totally, and even that was met with half success. He was lying more than sitting. And so still.

"I'll get you help," she told him, whispering as she fumbled to get the phone back on. There was no service, but she sent out the phone's SOS, meant to go through whenever it did come back on. It would put a tracking pin on their location and alert the authorities.

Eve glanced back down at Darius.

She knew she had taken a shot, but now she wondered if Darius had too. Or had the fall been enough?

"I'll get you help," she repeated.

A feeling of déjà vu mingled with her rising panic as she found the gun again and switched hands. The pain in her shoulder was starting to turn her stomach. Her side hurt too. So did her head.

Who was after them?

Why?

Was it Scott?

Was it people who worked for him?

Was it Gary's killer?

There was no time to figure it out.

Eve hovered in the cross-section of the pathways. She needed to get out to get help, but neither direction had light or sound coming from them. The way to the right might lead to the woods and an exterior exit…or it could dead end. For all the times her father had spoken about his work, Eve herself had never walked the mill to know for sure where every entrance and exit was.

The way to the left went in the direction of the heart of the steel mill… But wouldn't that mean the way out was probably farther away? And who was to say it was even accessible? Was where they were now even open to the general public, or had bad luck shown them a forgotten series of rooms?

There could be help in either direction, or there could be nothing, and Eve would have wasted Darius's time.

Eve turned back toward the way they had come.

Escaping into the darkness then had been about getting cover.

Now it was about getting out.

Eve flexed her grip around the butt of the gun. She tossed Darius's cell phone on the ground next to him.

"Don't die," she ordered him.

Then Eve ran full-tilt toward what she hoped was a good choice.

RAFE WAS DEAD. Dead as dead could be.

Lana moved along the old brick building and paused by its door, glancing in the direction of where the man lay prone. His gun, a thing that looked as old as the mill they had been circling, was at his side, but there were no signs he was going for it.

That man, that damned lawman, had gone and killed him true and through in one shot.

And her shot?

Well, Lana had been slower to it.

When she'd been asked to follow Detective Williams, she hadn't expected to find a Mrs. And when they had come all the way here, of all places? Lana thought it was better to keep at least one of them alive to get some answers.

That's the only reason she'd pulled her shot.

The reason the two had tucked into the building?

Lana saw the blood on the porch and guessed that for all Rafe was bad at, his first shot must have landed somewhere. But which one had taken it?

She didn't need to peek through the door to see if the couple were waiting for her right inside. The door was in pieces and gave a clear view of a confusing development.

The floor was gone.

Some of it, at least.

Lana held her gun out, ready to squeeze the trigger, and took a tentative step toward the hole in the hardwood. Sunlight from uncovered windows in the ground-level room gave just enough light to show there was an entirely different room hidden below. An old metal hunk of machinery could be seen at one side while a whole lot of nothing could be seen around the rest of the debris that had caved in.

The couple who had done the falling were nowhere to be seen.

Blood was, though.

That seemed to be the only easy thing to make out from her vantage point at the edge.

Lana held her breath. She cocked her head to the side a little.

No talking.

No rustling.

They had to have survived the fall, or else she would have seen their bodies. Maybe they were hiding in a part of the room she couldn't see?

Lana resisted the urge to sigh.

It would have been a whole lot nicer had Rafe not died.

She could have made him go down below and figure out their situation. But he had died the way he'd foolishly lived: impulsively.

That wasn't how Lana worked.

She kept her gun ready but lowered it to her side and looked around the rest of the aboveground space. She hadn't been there before but knew no one came around this part of the mill anymore. Whether they were paid to avoid it or just did it naturally, she didn't know or care. Her only job had been to follow, watch and report back.

Shoot if needed, only kill if you were told.

The room was large and open and looked to be a storage area that had been converted to hold several sleeping spaces. Rusted and broken iron bunk beds were positioned throughout the back end of the space. Nearest her seemed to have been a more general hangout spot. A couch that hadn't fallen below sagged low against the wall to her left. The wall to the right had a fogged window that looked out at another building in the distance.

She wasn't sure what building that was and, honestly, didn't care.

What she needed to do was figure out if the detective was still alive.

Lana was light and cautious with her steps around the opening in the floor until she made it to the back end of the main room. There were two closed doors, and both complained with metallic whines as she opened them.

The smell of mold hung heavy in the communal bathroom behind the first. The second held more of the same but with an added slight rot, which made sense considering it was a small, obviously forgotten kitchen. In neither room was there a set of stairs or another door that could lead to the room below.

Knowing there wasn't a back door, Lana opened a window over the sink. She climbed through it with ease and walked along the back wall of the building.

There were no stairs or exterior way to enter whatever room her mark had fallen into. At least not that she could see.

Lana turned toward the fence and the woods just beyond it. Would there be an access point there, or would she have to go in the other direction?

Maybe there wasn't an access point at all.

The mill was old, most of it repurposed instead of replaced as far as she had seen. They weren't in the working part either. Maybe they had closed up whatever they hadn't needed in order to skirt any liability issues.

Not that she cared.

She shouldn't have accepted the job to come to a place like Seven Roads.

Lana gave up her search for an easier way into whatever pit had formed beneath the detective's feet and instead looped back to the front door. When she went back inside, she holstered her gun and took a more conclusive look at her obstacle. She pulled her cell phone out and turned the flashlight function on. It didn't do much, but she could now guess the drop was about eight feet down. There didn't seem to be anything to help with that descent either, at least not from its concrete floor up to her.

Lana glanced around the dorm room around her. An industrial complex surely had something she could use to get down there without having to scale around like an acrobatic. Rope or a ladder or maybe if she could push one of the bunk-bed frames over the edge she could use it to drop onto and then climb back out of. Or maybe—

Lana had moved her gaze back to the hole as she went through potential plans.

The beam of light that was faint but clear enough was still empty. However, all thoughts stuttered to a stop when she realized that just outside of its scope was something she hadn't seen before.

At first, she thought it was the detective, but the shape was all wrong. Smaller.

The woman, she realized.

Not only had the woman survived a potential shot from Rafe and the fall, she had managed to collect a gun in the process.

And that gun was aimed up and right at Lana.

Her words carried with absolute clarity despite the open floor between them.

"Throw me your clip and then your gun or I'll shoot," she yelled up. "You've got ten seconds."

The woman was covered in dirt and blood. Her clothes were torn. Her hair a mess.

Her words were stone.

Despite herself, Lana was impressed.

But she was no fool.

The woman was at a disadvantage no matter how determined her voice sounded.

However, Lana wasn't going to test her patience.

She threw herself backward as far as she could.

No sooner than she lost sight of the hole than three gunshots shot out from it.

Lana might have stayed to see if she could run out the woman's clip, but another sound had entered the area.

Someone was coming. Their footfalls were loud in the silence that followed the last gunfire.

If there was someone other than her and Rafe, Lana hadn't been told about them. Which meant she wasn't going to take her chances that the detective or his woman had had the chance to call in backup.

Lana didn't sigh as she backtracked with quiet speed. She only handled problems that were listed in her contract. Whoever that woman was hadn't been on that list.

Though, as she disappeared into the woods behind the mill, she bet she would be soon.

Until then, Lana did what she did best.

She disappeared.

Chapter Eleven

Something had gone wrong.

It was the first thought Darius had before he opened his eyes, and it was only reinforced when he took in the room around him.

He was at the hospital.

Well, *in* the hospital.

A dull pain radiated up his left arm. A little pinch at his hand too. He couldn't see the bag or its label at the top of the IV pole, but he recognized the sound of digital monitors beeping. Over the last seven years or so, members of the McCoy County Sheriff's Department had been in and out of the hospital multiple times because of one case or another.

The hospital staff already knew most of them from living in such a confined area, but by now most had gone from a polite *hello* to the doctors and nurses to an easy first-name-basis chat.

However, in the last seven years, Darius hadn't been a patient. Only a visitor and a detective on the job.

He'd never been a patient who had, he guessed, gone through some sort of surgery. Darius looked down his left side. Instead of wearing a shirt, there were various bandages stuck to and wrapped around his arm, chest and shoulder.

He also guessed his ribs had a wrap, but he couldn't confirm it visually. A blanket was wrapped around him.

On top of that blanket a hand rested on his thigh.

There was a small bandage and tape holding an IV to the back of the hand. Darius followed the tube with his eyes until he had to turn his head slightly to his right. Someone was in the hospital bed with him, body pressed along the side of his, head laid back with the incline of the bed, and mouth wide open.

Darius must have been coming off some medication.

It took him way too long to worry about Eve.

He was glad that once his brain caught up to worry, she was already there with him.

She was resting above his blankets and wearing a hospital gown that stopped at her calves. Her rainbow socks were gone.

Darius continued tracing the plastic tube from her IV to the metal pole standing on the other side of the bed. He moved his head slightly to get a better view of the reason she needed it in the first place.

Eve had been shot. He knew the moment it happened because a pain he had never known before tore through him the second she had fallen against him. It wasn't until he had been in the room below the residence hall that he had guessed the same bullet had gone into him too.

He hadn't cared then. He didn't care now either.

Bandages peeked out of the top of Eve's gown, but he couldn't get a good view of how much of her was covered. Darius's own IV tube pulled as he gently moved the collar of her gown away a little.

There were no ulterior motives in the move—simply the need to see proof that it wasn't as bad as he had imagined at the time.

Eve didn't stir at the adjustment.

However, someone else did.

Theo stood from a chair near the foot of the hospital bed. There was a couch on the wall next to them. It was occupied by another sleeping woman. Winnie had a blanket wrapped around her.

Theo had a look of panic wrapped around him.

He put his finger to his lips and hurried over to Darius's side.

"Literally both of them just fell asleep," Theo whispered, so close that Darius could smell coffee on the boy's breath. "If you can, keep it down."

Normally, Darius would have been a little grumpy at the command, but it was obvious what had happened wasn't exactly normal. Darius took his advice to heart. He turned his head slowly, trying not to move Eve in the process. He waited a beat to make sure he succeeded in the attempt.

He only spoke once he confirmed her breathing was even.

"What time is it?"

Darius's mouth was dry. His throat hurt a little too. He managed to keep his voice low despite the uncomfortable feeling.

Theo didn't need to look at his phone or find a clock.

"Just after three in the morning. You've been out since yesterday." He frowned. "You lost a lot of blood. You had to have surgery too." His finger hovered next to the bandage on Darius's shoulder. "They had to dig a bullet out of you."

Darius understood why he was running slower now. He really was medicated. It explained the haze and the dull pain.

"I'm guessing they got it out?"

Theo nodded.

He pointed to Darius's side.

"You have some pretty intense bruising around there—we guess where you took the impact from the fall through the floor—and there's also some bad gashes around your thigh area. But other than where you were shot, there's no stitches. At least, the doctor didn't tell us if there were."

When he said the word *us*, his gaze went to Winnie on the couch.

Darius waited for him to look back before asking the part of the situation he didn't understand.

"What about her? Eve. Is she okay?"

Theo nodded again.

"The bullet that lodged into you went through her first, but she got lucky at the angle," he said. "It went clear through and didn't do any permanent damage. The doctor even clocked her recovery time at a few weeks as long as she takes her antibiotics."

Anger seared through Darius.

Eve being shot hadn't been *lucky* in his book.

Not at all.

"The man who did it?" he asked, jaw clenching.

Theo lowered his voice just a bit more.

"Died instantly. Never had a chance to shoot his gun again."

It hadn't been the first time Darius had had to take a life in the line of duty. That didn't mean he was used to it. But seeing as how the man had made the first move—that move being to shoot Eve—he wasn't overly upset about it.

"What about the second shooter? The woman."

"A woman carjacked Mr. Gleason at the gas station next to the mill around the time I got down to you and Eve. They caught her on camera and have an APB out on her and the car." He shook his head. "So far nothing, but the entire department is on it."

The last thing Darius remembered before blacking out was being in the dark with Eve in a tunnel beneath the residence hall. His eyebrow raised in question.

"When you got down to us?"

Theo went from frowning to brandishing a sheepish smile. He pulled at his earlobe in a fidgeting gesture.

"I kind of followed you yesterday morning."

Darius almost tilted his head to the side at that.

"You followed us... What do you mean?"

Eve had gone back out of his bedroom window the morning before while Darius had gone through the house, acting like everything was normal. He hadn't seen Theo at all.

That sheepish smile grew a little.

"Winnie convinced me to run a half-marathon with her in a few months, so I've been training before breakfast. I was out running and came back in time to see a lady coming out of your window. I almost said something until I realized it was Miss Myers. I, uh, hid to see what she was up to. Then when you came out and got into your truck with her... I got curious." His smile dropped. "I would have gotten to you sooner, but by the time I got out to the road, I had to guess where you'd gone. I guessed the right direction, and when I heard the first shots, I was close enough to the back-road turn. Sorry."

Darius wasn't sure why he was apologizing.

He said as much.

"It sounds like I should be thanking you. I'm guessing the second shooter took off because you showed up. You get us out of that room too?"

Theo looked pleased, even though he shook his head.

"I called Dad and EMTs before going down there to

check on you." He motioned in Eve's direction. "I tried to get her out first, but she refused to even try until you could come with her. Lucky for all of us that Rose's husband was close to us. He was the one who helped get you up the ladder we got from the main building."

James was Seven Roads's only mechanic. He was also a muscled mountain of a man. If there was anyone who could get Darius as dead weight up a ladder, it was definitely him.

Still, he didn't overlook what had been Theo's obvious effort.

"Thank you," Darius said, "for helping to get us."

Theo's cheeks turned a little red. He waved a dismissive hand through the air.

"Just trying to be a good tenant to my landlord is all. It was no biggie."

They finally got to the part of the conversation that was, indeed, a biggie. Darius knew that Theo felt it too. He cleared his throat but managed to stay as quiet as he had been.

His gaze moved to Eve.

"She wouldn't tell me—or anyone—why you two were there at the steel mill," he said. "All she would say is that you were the one who needed to answer the questions. Dad got mad at her, but I think that was more because of Scott Keys."

Darius felt that anger rise in him again.

Before they had been attacked, he had finally put together that Eve wasn't interested in Mitchell but rather his brother.

And not in a romantic way.

He hadn't had time to consider what was actually going on.

"Scott Keys? What was he doing?"

Theo rolled his eyes.

"Kicking up a fuss so loud that Dad and Blake had to pull in some lawyers."

That didn't make sense. Why was Scott kicking up a fuss at the sheriff when it seemed like the sheriff was the one also trying to find the bad guy? Theo must have picked up on the question. He answered it without Darius having to ask. Though, there was some hesitation in it.

"Mr. Keys seems to think that Miss Myers has an intimate relationship with you...and that's causing some issues."

Darius felt his eyes widen.

"An intimate relationship," he repeated.

Theo nodded.

"And he doesn't even know about the whole sneaking-out-of-your-window thing yesterday morning either."

It was Darius's turn to roll his eyes.

"I'm not having an affair with Eve," he started. "And even if I were, us getting attacked at the steel mill while there's still a homicide investigation going on doesn't really fit into a sexy rendezvous scenario, does it?"

"That's what Dad said too, but Mr. Keys still seemed pretty mad. Winnie pulled me back to the waiting room while they left to go to the department, so I'm not sure how that all resolved. No one has been here to see either one of you except us and Mitchell since visiting hours ended."

In all the information dump, Darius had forgotten to wonder where Eve's fiancé—real or fake—currently was.

And why Eve herself was in *his* bed.

Thankfully, Theo kept his answering streak going.

"Miss Myers's room is next door, and Mitchell Keys was in there sleeping last I saw. She said that he knew where she was when she came in here an hour or so ago and that it was okay." That sheepish look came back. "I worried about her getting into bed with you and also that Mr. Keys would be mad, but Miss Myers told me something that made Winnie give me The Look. You know, the don't-ask-any-more-questions look. They fell asleep not too long after that."

Darius noted the boy's cheeks had reddened again.

"She said something *to you*, the pragmatic one, that made you think it was okay for her to hop into my hospital bed while we *both* are injured and one of us in engaged to a very rich, well-connected man?" Darius had a hard time with that one. Winnie he could see letting it slide because she had, no doubt, picked up on the fact that Darius and Eve were close.

Or *had* been close.

But Theo?

He usually took a lot more convincing. Which was why Darius wasn't surprised or all that offended that the boy had followed them the day before.

Now he shrugged a little and nodded to Eve.

"She said you were hers," he said, matter-of-factly. "And between us, she was very convincing."

THE YOUNG MAN named Theo had a nice voice that would have been good for narrating books or hosting podcasts. At first, Eve accepted his whisper-talking in tandem with Darius's deep drone like it was white noise.

Which was good, considering she felt she was still in need of a mighty nap.

Only when that white noise became words she could follow did she remember where she was.

And who had finally woken up.

Excitement nearly made Eve open her eyes to detail out as much of Darius as she could before slinging a barrage of questions his way. How was he feeling? Did his shoulder hurt? What about his side? Did he want water? Did he need a doctor?

She managed to keep the desire to a thought only.

She liked Theo for what he had done, but Eve still wasn't ready to let him into the secret.

The secret she was finally ready to tell Darius, despite swearing to keep him and anyone else out of it.

While the two men spoke quietly at her side, Eve took a chance and moved slightly. When no one reacted, she used her hand's new position to place her thumb against Darius's leg. She applied a quick three pulses of pressure.

The man didn't move a muscle.

Did he not get the hint?

A few moments passed by, Eve readied to do it again, but Darius apparently had understood the assignment.

"Hey, why don't you go ahead and take Winnie home?" he said when their conversation paused. "I know for a fact that those couches are uncomfortable as all get-out, and since I'm clearly okay now, there's no reason for her to suffer on it and for you to do the same on a chair."

There was some initial pushback at the suggestion. That pushback doubled when Winnie herself was woken. It was obvious that neither of them wanted to leave, but eventually Darius won out with a compromise. They would leave for only a little while, get some sleep and be back as soon as visiting hours started again.

No discussions happened past that.

Theo and Winnie said hushed good-byes before their quiet footfalls finally left the room.

The second the door closed, Eve opened her eyes.

It was no surprise that Darius was already looking at her.

"Climbing through windows and climbing into beds,"

he said. "I'm almost scared to see what habit you'll pick up next."

Eve suppressed an eye roll.

Mainly because there had been a specific reason why she was there now. It wasn't just concern.

It was necessity.

And she cut right to the chase.

"We need to get our stories on the same page right now," she said.

Darius's dark brow rose.

"About the real reason you're with Mitchell Keys," he guessed.

She nodded.

"And why I think it's time I officially ask for your help."

Chapter Twelve

"I kind of lied about why we left Seven Roads when we were kids."

Eve was staring at the wall across from them. The hospital room's TV had been off since Darius had been wheeled in after his surgery. No one had thought to turn it on after, even on low. Darius had never been someone who could sit in front of a TV with any real enthusiasm. He was more of a book or hands-on-project kind of guy. He had never been much of a fan of noise.

If Eve had to guess, she thought those ways of his hadn't exactly changed over the years. He was single, living in his childhood home, working a job that forced him to ask more questions than answer. The only surprise was that he had taken on a roommate. Though, the younger man also seemed prone to talking less than more. At least until the young woman, Winnie, was in the room.

The three of them had spoken quietly earlier beneath the TV no one had even thought to turn on.

Then again, who was Eve to say if Darius had or hadn't changed since they were kids? She had been gone.

Did people really change all that much from when they were kids?

Circumstances forced action—but change? Real change?

It was a question Eve had wondered throughout the years, usually in the quiet of the night, staring at the bedroom ceiling and trying to remember the little girl who had once lived in Seven Roads.

Now Eve let out a breath. This was a story she needed to tell him—she knew that—but that didn't mean she was eager to do it.

Regardless of her feelings, Darius gave her the space to work through them. He was quiet as she tried to figure out the best entry point to the origin of her lie.

He didn't even question why she was sharing his hospital bed.

He didn't say anything at all.

Eve had already heard a bit of gossip in town about people often calling him cold.

That she didn't understand.

Darius Williams had always been warm to her.

It was one of the reasons she hadn't wanted to leave Seven Roads as a kid.

It was one of the reasons a part of her was glad to finally be able to explain why she had.

Eve adjusted her gaze to the spot across the room where the wall met the ceiling. Her memory yanked her back into the past.

"I didn't know Dad was sick until we were in Texas," she started, eyes straight ahead. "Maybe because he was never really at the house because of work when we were here, or maybe because, by the time he did start to hang around after Mom left, I was so used to being by myself I just didn't see the signs. So when we got to Houston and he told me he'd been accepted into a drug study—his last chance at surviving—our life here in Seven Roads just kind of disappeared."

Eve picked at the fabric of her hospital gown.

She didn't like hospitals, doctors or medical clinics, but over the last decade or so, she had more than gotten used to them.

"I won't get too into the details because he's okay now, but back then, even with the drug trial, he was really sick," Eve continued. "You know Mom, once she left here that was it for us as a family. And remember Aunt Pat? She'd just had her third kid. The rest of Dad's family wasn't exactly dependable to start with either. So when things started getting really bad, I realized it would be just me taking care of Dad."

There was still an anxiety there. An imprint of the terror in Eve's chest when she finally understood that the position of sole caregiver would have to go to her. That her father dying wasn't something she could avoid or ignore. That she couldn't simply give him encouragement or a hug as she passed by. That the man she had barely seen because of his work throughout her young life was now the person who needed her most.

And it had all happened so quickly too.

One week she had been climbing through Darius's window, a lonely but happy preteen, the next she was standing in a small apartment in Texas with a father who was staring at death, asking her to hold his hand.

"We finally started getting really promising results around the time I turned sixteen," Eve continued. "When I was eighteen, Dad was given the all clear. He still has to take meds for the rest of his life, but the shortened life expectancy we'd kept hearing about every year was finally extended."

For the first time in years, he had been smiling too. It

had been better than any present Eve could have gotten for officially becoming an adult.

At the same time, that happiness had seesawed with a new, uncomfortable weight.

"But by that point, it had been almost eight years," she said. "Eight years of me taking care of him. Of always being on call. Being there every minute I could. Chores and exercise. Tracking medicines and making doctor visits. Having to deal with financial problems, picking up after-school jobs to help fill the gap."

Eight years of a childhood that hadn't been childlike at all.

Eight years of realizing that the only taste of a childhood she'd had at all was because of the man sitting next to her now.

"So when it was time to graduate high school and head to college, I couldn't just leave." Guilt mingled in with the feeling of being medicated. It was an old, worn and beaten kind of shame. The shame of a lie told so much that, at times, Eve had forgotten it was a lie at all. "I didn't tell Dad that's why I decided not to go to college. He'd just started dating for the first time since Mom left and was trying to find some normal… So I lied and told him I'd rather work."

Waitressing, tending bar, seasonal cashier jobs, odds-and-ends gigs like cleaning and babysitting. Just anything and everything she could do to help with the bills and debt that had piled up Eve did for the next ten years.

"It wasn't until Dad got remarried to my stepmom and moved out of that small apartment that I really realized we had finally done it. We'd gotten him out of this exhausting situation where it felt like he'd been trying to climb out of some never-ending hole for years. But that's when I really understood the part I'd really played in helping him get out of it."

Eve sighed.

"I hadn't pulled him out, I'd pushed him out. Which meant I was still there when he was able to finally walk away." She listed her next points lazily off on the fingers still resting against Darius's leg. "I had no real friends, no real career, no life goal or dreams I was running toward. My romantic relationships came down to a handful of dates scattered between weekend shifts and overtime, and even though I managed to get an apartment that wasn't all that bad, it was just a place I went to for sleep."

Eve snorted, a bit of self-loathing in the sound.

It was another feeling she never would forget.

Over thirty years old and she felt like she was a kid again, standing at the beginning of adulthood without a clue about what to do first.

The spot on the wall Eve had been staring at blurred slightly.

She cleared her throat and continued.

"I tried to slow down after that," she said. "I tried making friends, find a relationship that meant something, figure out career things and if I even had dreams. Then, through one of Dad's old friends he'd made from his treatment days, I learned about some work the Keys Foundation had done with a medical project in a small town in Alabama. I checked their social media and found a press release about Scott Keys, praising small-town medical studies. When he named-dropped the hospital's new research annex that was in Seven Roads—well, I was sure it was fate."

"I applied for a job at the foundation's headquarters in Atlanta, got an interview and probably was the most excited I had been in years." Eve laughed, but it was short and not at all humorous. "Though, with my résumé, or lack thereof, they told me on the spot that I wasn't a good fit. Now, believe me, I understand their reasoning. I was underqualified for sure. But to go all that way, just to be told I wasn't good enough? It was rough."

The small hope Eve had had?

It had disappeared into the night air then.

"I went to the bar later, ready to drown my sorrows in drinks I couldn't really afford, when I ran into a group of guys being rowdy in a nearby alley. Three guys against one, and the one guy who was being pushed around didn't look like he could hit a wet paper bag stuck on the sidewalk."

At this part, Eve felt a smile curve up the corner of her lips. It was genuine.

Darius finally spoke.

"Let me guess. You jumped in to help the one," he said.

Eve laughed a little. She nodded.

"I went in there all loud and fast—you know, not giving them a second to really think—and finally made enough space to get the guy and run." If it had been a movie, their escape would have been in slow motion Eve had thought even then. Dramatic but fun. Low stakes that, in the moment, had felt so high. "Once we were clear of them, he treated me to a nice meal that I was in no mood to refuse. We chatted all night before I had to go back to my hotel and we'd had a good time, but there were no plans to see each other again or talk, even. So when I got a call early the next morning to come in for another interview with the Keys Foundation, I was surprised as all get-out to see him there. Standing all smart and proper in a suit."

"Mitchell Keys," Darius guessed.

Eve nodded.

"Mitchell had gone back that night after our dinner and

told Scott about my so-called daring rescue. Scott had wanted to meet me before I left town, so what I thought was an interview with HR for a job at their headquarters ended up being a meal with the big boss himself. Before that meal was even finished, he hired me to be his personal assistant." At the time, Eve had been so surprised her mouth had flopped open like a fish out of water. It had been the first bit of hope she'd had in years. "Scott said I was good under pressure, and if I could handle an issue like that with his brother discreetly, then working with a high-profiler like himself would be easy. So I became his assistant."

Again if it had been a movie, that would have been the beginning of a beautiful ending.

Down-on-her-luck, listless daughter finally finds purpose and drive again. Meets not one but two kind men who care. Finds purpose in work, love and life.

Life fulfilled.

Future bright.

But that wasn't what happened next.

There was no need to pad the rest of the past with emotional asides and deep, life-changing epiphanies.

Now Eve was at the fact portion of her problems.

"Out of all the work that Scott did, I took the most interest in his involvement in anything medical, and when he started meeting with a man named Horace Clare, owner of Clare Biometrics, I couldn't help but pay attention."

"Clare Bio," Darius echoed. His low rumble vibrated against her as he spoke. "The company that's about to use the research annex here for a new pharmaceutical trial? I didn't know that the Keys Foundation had anything to do with them. I've only heard Scott wanted to invest in the town, but not how."

Eve nodded.

"He's been looking into ways to boost the economy by bringing in new business, using the research annex and whatever study they do as a good example of how small towns can do big things."

"His whole Small Town White Knight shtick."

She nodded again.

"I thought his meetings with Horace were related to Clare Bio being the new company to move into the research annex," Eve continued. "And that it was all happy coincidence that I, his new assistant, had lived in the same town as a kid. I was wrong."

Eve finally turned face the man next to her. Darius did the same. His brow was drawn in.

"Scott had been interested in Seven Roads before he met me, before he met Horace and way before he made it known publicly that he was investing in the town."

Darius's eyebrow rose high.

"What? Why?"

Eve lowered her voice, glancing at the closed door just past him.

"I think he's been the reason behind all of the town's problems these past few years."

Darius also glanced at the door. When his gaze was back on her, he looked as cold as the town rumors claimed.

"What do you mean all our problems? Do you mean our past cases? Because, as much as I'd like to blame one person for all of them, even the big investigations we've gone through over the last few years have been cut-and-dried once we got all our ducks in a row."

Eve had known about the department's big cases over the last decade simply because she had been keeping tabs on a certain detective's career. At least, for the most part.

That task had become much easier thanks to a few key investigations and their outcomes making the national news.

That's why Eve hadn't intended on telling Darius, or anyone else, her discovery until she had concrete evidence. Her belief, her accusation, would change everything. Without proof, though? She knew she sounded delusional.

Staring now at a man who had a successful career as a detective in part because of these past wild cases, she felt some nerves start to twist in her stomach.

She wiggled a little like the physical move could dislodge the new feeling.

It didn't.

She continued anyways.

There was no point in keeping it in any longer.

Darius had taken a bullet because of her.

The truth would hurt less.

She hoped.

"I think he's the reason he got the White Knight of Small-town Living nickname in the first place."

Darius's eyebrow lifted once more.

"He gave himself the nickname?"

Eve shook her head.

Her answer felt as loud in mostly dark hospital room as the gunshot had.

"I think Scott Keys destroys small towns just so he can save them." Eve made sure to hold Darius's gaze. He sure was handsome. She let out a small breath. "And I think he's only coming to save Seven Roads now…because he's spent the last several years slowly destroying it."

Chapter Thirteen

The town was in an uproar and, for the first time it had nothing to do with the danger or mystery that had taken place within its limits.

No one really cared about the still-unknown woman shooter who had carjacked Mr. Gleason while he was pumping premium or that, while his car had reappeared in the next county over, she hadn't.

No one seemed to care about the shooter who had died at the steel mill being identified as a Rafe Bailey—a do-anything for hire with a long jacket of various criminal activities and time spent in several county jails and one state prison—or the fact that still no one knew who had hired him.

And when it came to the steel mill itself—the largest employer of the entire town, and the one stretch of space in all of Seven Roads that most residents had been to at least once—almost no one spoke about the boarded-up, blocked-off and hidden network of old rooms beneath that had been partially discovered after the shooting.

Some did speak to the fact that the shooting in question had resulted in the injuries of the only McCoy County detective and the Keyses' almost-bride, but most of those people chattering were working at the sheriff's department.

One of their own had been hurt, and they had no one in custody to answer for it. A gnawing problem that kept their focus on the things that mattered most.

Talk of Gary Whittaker's homicide case, still without a lead, hadn't completely died down, but the shock value's stock had never risen too high to begin with, since he had been an outsider.

Instead, the gossip that blew every other piece of news out of the water for the town locals kept to one bit of information that had leaked in the aftermath of all the hubbub.

The rumored breakup of Evelyn Myers and Mitchell Keys.

It was one thing for the wedding to be postponed because of a homicide. But for the bride-to-be to be caught out with another man the day after with no public explanation, not to mention the extra layer of rumor that Scott Keys had made such a stink at the sheriff's department, demanding that same man be fired... Who cared about Gary Whittaker?

Who cared about the missing shooter?

Who cared why there had been a shooting at all?

Darius, a week later, believed he could have left the town in ruins if they could only see who met him in his living room after finally being released from the hospital.

Eve, sitting cross-legged in front of a laptop on his couch, nearly fell over as she tried to undo herself to stand. Mitchell, sitting next to her, managed to catch the water bottle she'd had sitting next to her before it fell to the floor.

"I didn't think you were getting released until this afternoon," Eve exclaimed, righting herself. Mitchell gave her a little push for extra stability. She didn't address it. Her gaze went over his shoulder to the hallway leading to the front door. "How did you get here? Did you drive? Is that allowed? I mean, I know it's mainly the one side of you that's all hurt, but surely that's still not allowed. You know, I got a flu shot in the backside once, and it hurt like all heck just driving back a few blocks, so I bet a bullet wound would—"

Darius held up one hand in a *stop* gesture and interrupted the raging flow of thoughts.

"Theo's outside with my bag," he said. "He'll be in after he finishes telling Liam I'm out and home. My phone's juice is low, or else I'd do it."

He added in the last part because he had a feeling Eve was about to grill him on why he hadn't called her.

Which would have been another awkward exchange in front of her fiancé if it weren't for the fact that both had already set the story straight for him back at the hospital.

"The fight that Eve helped rescue me from when we first met was with my ex-boyfriend's *new* boyfriend and his friends," Mitchell had explained, sitting on the couch next to Darius's hospital bed. "They were under the impression that I was trying to get back with him after we ran into each other earlier that day by accident. They accused me of using my money and influence to try and win him back. I…got a little heated at that, and that's when they remembered it was three against one."

Mitchell had shared a look with Eve that was clear in its gratitude. She'd accepted it from her spot on the edge of Darius's bed with a little nod.

Then Mitchell's attention had fastened on Darius again. There it had stayed for the remainder of his explanation.

"If that isn't an indication of the important part—I'm gay," he'd clarified. "But I've never come out to most of my family or the public, and so far I've managed to keep it a secret, despite people like those guys trying to make me pay for whatever imagined slights they think I've committed."

"So Scott doesn't know," Darius had had to make sure.

Mitchell had nodded.

"Our father was a very traditional man, who made it very clear that to inherit the family money and business an heir had to be just as traditional. While I've never been in the running for being the CEO or taking a seat on any board since Scott is older, my mother's deathbed wish was to make sure I at least inherited my share of the money when my father did pass. Which meant the easiest thing I could do was leave the idea of *traditional* on the table, at least for a few years." He'd sighed out long at that. "Those few years turned into over a decade, and then Dad got sick, and I realized the idea of not admitting who I am just to get money…felt too wrong to keep going. So I decided to finally come out, and I was so nervous that I invited one of the few friends I had over to help me practice what I was going to say."

Mitchell had been tensing slowly Darius had noticed. At that part, his shoulders had become a hard line of obvious stress.

"In hindsight I shouldn't have picked a hotel as a meeting place but we were working out of town so it seemed practical," he continued. "Scott saw me go into a room, with a man, and assumed we were there for other things. And when my friend left, Scott came in to—I thought—talk too."

Eve had balled her hand into a fist. Her jaw had tightened.

She'd been mad.

Darius had understood why after Mitchell stood, turned around, and lifted his shirt.

Scars—so many different lengths and depths and severity—had been spread across the skin of his back, a horrifying series of stamps of the past. Even Darius had felt his own anger rise at the sight.

"The mere idea that I had kept a secret from him, sent Scott into a rage," Mitchell had started again after a moment. He'd turned around, face fallen. "He didn't care if I was gay—he didn't even ask—but the thought that I might have been trying to 'scam him out' of what would have been all rightfully his? He was so angry that he didn't even give me a chance to confirm or deny if I dated men or not. If it wasn't for Eve, I'm not sure what would have happened had I actually told him the truth."

Eve's jaw had unclenched then.

"I had already been working for Scott for a while and saw him break from schedule," she'd jumped in. "I followed him, worried I'd somehow made a scheduling mistake, and when I realized what was happening, I said what I thought would be the most helpful in the moment—that Mitchell wasn't secretly dating men but secretly dating me instead."

"And, even though I had been planning on telling the truth up until then, I saw something in my brother that scared me to lie along with her." Mitchell had lowered his voice. It had made his next confession all the more sinister-sounding. "A man who would do anything and everything for power, for money, for status, even kill his own brother for even the chance of getting slightly more of it all."

Eve's expression had softened but her words were still as harsh as they had been before.

"I had just found out that the foundation had money coming out of and going into accounts I couldn't identify or trace when they should have been going into various originations, specifically the drug trial that during which my father's friend had died. I had been planning on asking, assuming it was some kind of clerical issue, but then I saw what he did to Mitchell. And how, even after I caught him in the act, he buttoned up like it was nothing after he accepted our lie. He even smiled."

Eve had shaken her head.

"So I opened up to Mitchell instead, and for the last six months, we've been doing our own investigation into the missing money, and *two* months ago we finally had a breakthrough."

"But before we could do anything with it, Scott told me I needed to marry Eve," Mitchell had added. "Not that I should or might want to, that I *had* to."

"Right when you two found something that might expose him," Darius had underlined.

They'd nodded in tandem.

"We're worried that he found something out but can't figure out what that might be," Eve had said.

"And we were worried Scott was setting us up somehow. Why else would he want me to marry all of a sudden?"

This was when Darius finally understood the lie Eve had told him the day of the wedding.

"Which is why I met with Gary Whittaker once before we came to Seven Roads," Mitchell had said, sheepish in his confession. "I wanted to know the full extent of what it meant for Eve and me to be married and what she would legally be able to do, wondering if there was a reason in there that we could find for the sudden rush down the aisle."

"It was like I lit a fire beneath him and asked him to sit on it," Mitchell had continued after a bewildered expression had crossed over his face. "He became angry and said he wouldn't answer any family questions without the family there—without Scott there. Which only made *me* panic, and I reeled everything back in and wrote it off as prewedding nerves. It seemed to calm him down, but then when I tried to talk to him last week, he looked like he was seeing a ghost."

"When you saw him last week," Darius had repeated.

The conspiratorial partners had glanced away from him at that.

Mitchell took his blame well despite it.

"I met Gary for lunch the day he was killed, just after noon."

Darius had looked at Eve for that. She'd met his gaze too, less enthused to admit her part in what had happened next.

"Which I didn't know about because I was too busy trying to stop the wedding, so when I was asked about where Mitchell was later… I lied and said I was with him."

The rest of the conversation had been short, but Darius couldn't deny he had felt something in him shift at finally knowing the why behind Eve's lie. It wasn't that she was in love with Mitchell or held him on some pedestal because of his fortune, status and connection to his older, much more popular brother.

She had been trying to help a friend.

A friend who swore up and down that Gary had been alive when he'd left his hotel room around twelve twenty.

There was no evidence or way to confirm Mitchell's story, but despite himself Darius believed him. Maybe, he realized, because Eve did.

After that, Darius might have stayed in the hospital, but Gary Whittaker's homicide case had done something he hadn't expected it to do.

It had gone backward.

Back before the day of the wedding, or the arrival of the wedding party in Seven Roads, or the engagement, or the lie told to Scott about Eve and Mitchell's secret relationship. Because, they might not have had proof yet, but

Darius had had a hard time believing it had been a coincidence that Gary had been killed after talking with Mitchell.

And, for the first time since the murder, Darius had a lead he knew would go somewhere.

It just was a matter of how to approach it.

Now standing in his living room and staring at the fake couple who had spent the last half of a year trying to topple a man steeped in money and power, Darius had a plan.

One it was time to share.

"You think Scott is using his money from the foundation to fund more sinister activities. I think you're right. And I've come up with a plan that I think will prove it."

Darius had spent the last several days in the hospital pouring over all the notes Eve and Mitchell had made on their investigation. Their breakthrough had been less of a breakthrough and more of a hunch that someone in the wedding party had helped with Scott's less-than-legal intentions.

As of that morning, Darius believed he'd finally bridged that hunch to what would be a tangible piece of evidence.

If they played their cards right.

Eve's eyes had widened as she waited for his explanation.

Instead, he knew he was about to get her anger next.

"But I'll only help on one condition." Darius pointed to the woman standing in front of him. "You don't leave my side. Not once and not for anything."

"What? Why?" Darius noted her reddening cheeks, but he didn't wait to see if it was from annoyance or something else.

Instead, he narrowed his eyes at her and made sure the aim of his finger stayed true.

"Because you, Evelyn Myers, have a talent for getting into trouble. Whether you're making it or falling into it. So until we get this entire thing settled, you aren't leaving my sights. Agree now, or else you two can leave and I'll let you figure it all out on your own."

That, of course, was a lie.

And like the fake alibi she'd given Darius before, he knew that *Eve* knew it was a lie too.

Still, she'd never been one with the personality to accept an ultimatum easily. Her nostrils flared a little as she took a moment to let his nonthreat linger.

Mitchell was smart enough to also stay quiet behind her.

Darius was finding that he was liking the man more and more.

After a moment, Eve let out a quick breath of defeat.

"Fine," she gave in. "Until we can prove the White Knight of Small-town Living is the villain in disguise, I'm all yours, Detective Williams."

Chapter Fourteen

Lunch was served by Theo, moving around the small kitchen with ease while bickering with the young woman named Winnie even more. They were talking about the best practices to train for a half-marathon one moment, and the next they were fussing about the proper way to make a sandwich worthy of a specialty shop.

Mitchell threw in his two cents worth from his spot at the kitchen counter about what he thought were the best trimmings for said perfect sandwich, and this, somehow, transitioned into a conversation about the local coffee shop. What constituted the perfect drink came next. Eve let her attention wander to the man sitting opposite her while their debate started.

Darius seemed uncomfortable.

And it wasn't with the current company chattering in his kitchen.

Something in him was hurting or, at least, bothering him. Eve had already seen him adjust his shoulder twice, and his drawn brow hadn't relaxed since he'd arrived home.

She couldn't blame him.

Not only had he been shot and gone through surgery and recovery in the hospital, he had also spent those days studying the chaotic notes Eve and Mitchell had taken on a story that, if broken, would at the very least turn the town upside-down.

Then he had come home and gone right to work.

There was no rest for the wicked; there was no rest for detectives who knew Eve Myers.

A problem that Eve understood was tricky.

What if she hadn't come back to Seven Roads, at least until they'd had concrete evidence of Scott's wrongdoings?

Darius wouldn't be sitting across from her, wounded and working in secret. Setting his rules, his procedures, aside for a case that wasn't even technically a case.

Because keeping everything on the down-low was the other stipulation that everyone in the kitchen had agreed upon.

Their deep dive into Scott Keys, the fake relationship between Eve and Mitchell and the connection to Gary Whittaker and his murder were all pieces of information that they alone knew about.

It was another point of pressure that Eve had inadvertently applied to her former boy next door.

She hadn't even asked him to keep such a complicated secret once he had taken her bullet. Yet the straight-as-an-arrow lawman had done so.

It made Eve's stomach twist a little. The memory of his one condition being that she couldn't leave his side—well, that made her stomach feel a different kind of way.

That feeling, and a sudden warmth crawling up her neck, made Darius's gaze suddenly pulling up to meet hers only intensify.

Eve tried to play it off.

She tapped the table's top beneath her finger.

"Out of all the furniture you got rid of from when we

were kids, I'm glad this one didn't make the cut," she tried.
"I've always liked this table."

Darius snorted.

"You only like this table because of how much my
mother loved it."

Eve couldn't deny that. She shrugged. The sandwiches
might not have been finished, but Winnie had clearly decided it was time to enter a more interesting conversation.
She was smiling as she sat down to Eve's right, her back
against the wall so she could keep an eye on Theo's progress, Eve assumed.

"Theo said you two were neighbors," she said. "I didn't
realize you were close to Darius's parents too."

At this Darius's snort turned into a little chuckle.

Winnie's smile faded a bit. It probably didn't help that
Eve must have looked offended.

"Close in distance but never in spirit," she clarified.
"My time spent in this house was out of sight and mind
of those two."

Winnie's eyebrow rose as Theo started to hand out plates
of food. Mitchell joined him. He looked as perplexed as
they did.

"But you like this table because his mother loved it?"
Theo repeated. "Doesn't that imply that you feel a fondness for her since she felt a fondness for it?"

Darius let out a bite of laughter again but decided to
help out.

He tapped the table's top.

"Put on your phone's flashlight and look underneath."

Winnie, Theo and Mitchell did just that.

Mitchell was the one to read the words that had been
scratched into the wood in little-kid handwriting.

"Eve Myers owns this table. Jon D. can bite tires."

Three faces emerged with varying expressions of delight and confusion.

Eve thought it was telling of their personalities who asked the following questions.

"You wrote this?" Mitchell asked. "How old were you?"

Eve didn't have to think long.

"I was a persistent eight-year-old, who thankfully got a little better with my handwriting."

Winnie was next.

"You claimed the table as yours because you *didn't* like his mother," she said. "Did she ever see this?"

Darius answered that with a resounding *no*.

"For almost two years she sat at this table never knowing that little Eve the terror had defamed one of her favorite pieces of furniture."

Theo only seemed concerned about the last part.

"Who's Jon D. and why can he *bite tires*?" he asked.

At this Darius's mouth shut and thinned into a line.

In all honesty, Eve had forgotten she had added in a mention of Jon D. Even before what he'd done when they were ten, she had already greatly disliked the boy. She sobered a little for her answer, trying to be as discreet as possible. She might not have been around for the last twenty years or so, but she had a feeling that Darius hadn't been chatty about the origin of the scar on his back.

The scar on her own hand felt oddly heavy as she answered.

"He was a boy who lived down the street and who only came during the summer breaks to stay with his grandparents," she explained. "He decided to make it his personal mission every summer to make our lives miserable. Around the time I scratched that in, he was at a level seven out of ten on the annoyance scale. If you'd given me a few years I'd have written in a lot worse."

Darius didn't add anything to that.

The rest of the table seemed to take the hint. They fell into a communal silence as each ate their food. It wasn't until a few contented sighs and the sight of empty plates later that the silence was broken.

Eve was the one to do it.

"So how do we prove that Scott has been destroying small towns before he saves them? What did you find that we didn't?"

Everyone's gaze waved over to the man at the head of the table.

Darius didn't flinch at the dramatic, yet valid, questions. Instead, he seemed more than ready for them.

"You and Mitchell built your investigation on timing, right? Scott meeting with key individuals in one town before and after something inherently goes wrong, only to be able to fix that exact thing that went wrong." Eve nodded, not that he needed the confirmation. Her notes had looked like a madwoman's rantings and ravings as she had tracked Scott over the past ten years as best she could through financial transactions, planners, press releases and gossip.

"There was a lot of overlap of him being at the scene of the crime before the crime happened and then directly after," she confirmed.

"Like what's been happening with Clare Biometrics," Winnie added.

Eve had been the one to personally tell Winnie and Theo everything she knew, while Darius had been in the hospital. However, she was starting to realize that Winnie had a knack for making sure everyone was on the same page. It seemed to be a trait that Theo appreciated too.

Eve nodded.

"The last pharmaceutical company that had used the research annex, Camden Pharmaceuticals, was ruined by corruption, and after the investigations and the company being shut down and having to leave, the whole thing was a big hit against Seven Roads and the county's future growth. Until Horace took an interest in it and decided to go on contract with Clare Biometrics for the next ten years," Eve said. "Horace Clare coming to town created excitement and created a positive outlook for Seven Roads, which is what Scott claims had *him* become interested in the town."

"Which seems harmless until you realize that Scott had met with one of the higher-ups of Camden Pharmaceuticals twice before they moved to Seven Roads," Mitchell added.

"Which, again, might not seem like anything if you look at it as an isolated event, but of the three small towns that Scott has been praised for supposedly saving, there have been similar situations like this," Eve added.

It was Darius's turn to nod. He domed his fingers on top of the table.

"The breakthrough you and Mitchell say you made right before Scott insisted on the two of you getting married was finding the flight plans for Scott's best friend, Toby Sanderson," he underlined.

Mitchell and Eve confirmed that.

"We realized from the big uproars that happened in the second small town he was praised with saving that Scott hadn't met with anyone but his best friend and fellow rich socialite Toby Sanderson had," she said. "And he'd gone there on his private jet. We had finally gotten our hands on a copy of those flight records when Scott told Mitchell to propose."

"Then Mitchell reached out to Gary Whittaker about the

legal side of being married, since he was the family law-yer," Darius said. He looked to Winnie and Theo. While he had agreed, begrudgingly, to let them in on what was happening, he hadn't been able to talk to them at the hospital for any real length of time.

Theo let him know that this information was something that they already knew.

"Which seemed to freak Mr. Whittaker out," Theo finished.

"A feeling he still had when Mitchell went to meet with Gary the day of the wedding," Winnie said. "Right before he was killed *somewhere* within an hour-and-a-half radius of the diner here in town where he and Mitchell met."

Despite their harrowing time spent at the steel mill, the site of Gary's murder was still a mystery, as was his killer.

Darius moved his hand to tap the top of the table, bringing their attention back to him.

"So let's assume that finding the flight plans and linking Toby Sanderson to Scott's plans alerted Scott in some way, leading him to force Mitchell to marry Eve—though, I'd like to point out we aren't sure that's what happened because the motive there is unclear," Darius started. "Meeting with the family lawyer only for him to be killed right after seems like too much of a coincidence given our original assumption. I think that either Gary knew something about Scott that he shouldn't have known, or Scott believed that Mitchell told Gary something he shouldn't have known. And then suddenly two guns-for-hire come for me and Eve the next day?"

Darius shook his head.

"I think there's a disconnect between the two sides of what we all assume is connected to the White Knight of Small-town Living," he continued. "Scott doesn't know what Mitchell has found out and, like us, is probably only making guesses and reacting to opportunities as fast as he can."

He paused long enough to jab the tabletop once, but that was enough to make what he said next the star of the show.

"So I want us to make an opportunity of our own that will make him so nervous he'll be forced to react," he said. "Then he's ours."

THE PLAN TO entrap a millionaire savior by using his best friend to admit to a conspiracy that had been at least ten years in the making wasn't all that complicated.

The sleeping arrangements that night, however, were.

At least they felt that way to Darius, who'd spent more minutes than he should have staring at his closet before his shower. He chose a full outfit for his sleepwear, a black T-shirt and some sweatpants, and took care to make sure each piece was perfectly in place after slipping into bed once his bandages had been changed and his medicine had been taken.

Theo helped with the latter part of the routine, hanging around in Darius's bedroom until he was satisfied that he had helped enough. Then he went to the living room and, Darius had no doubt, instantly went to sleep on the couch. Apparently, he hadn't been getting that much sleep while Darius was in the hospital. Darius made note that, once everything was said and done, he would have to do something for the boy. Winnie too. They might have been young, but they could give most of the adults he'd met in his life a run for their money when it came to being considerate.

A good example of that was Theo giving his room to Eve for the night.

Something she had lightly huffed about.

"I don't want to put you out," she'd told Theo after Winnie had left and Mitchell was wrapping up to go too.

Theo had waved the thought off. Mitchell had offered to get him a room at the hotel where he was staying—and where Eve had, in name, also been staying—but Theo had refused to leave Darius, still hurt, alone.

Though, there was never any real danger in that worry.

He'd made it clear that Eve wasn't going to leave his side and she had been just as vocal about staying put. Her suitcase had already been in his room when he'd come back from the hospital.

Now that suitcase was down the hall in his childhood bedroom.

And Darius was staring up at the ceiling, wondering if the anxiousness he was feeling in him was warranted or not.

Half an hour after the house quieted and he was searching for the sleep that was trying to elude him, Darius was silently grateful for his thinking ahead about his sleepwear choice.

The bedroom door didn't squeak, but the floorboard just outside of it did.

Darius kept his eyes closed as the soft clicks of the door opening and closing preceded the soft shuffles of feet wrapped in socks.

He still didn't open his eyes when the mattress sank lightly beside him a few moments later.

Eve took care not to touch him this time, though she did speak.

"Let me stay for a bit," she whispered at his shoulder. "It feels weird to sleep in this house without you."

Because he knew Eve, Darius understood the statement was innocent in nature. She had, after all, spent most of her nights asleep in the same house with him next to her on the floor as kids.

But also because he knew Eve, Darius understood something else the moment she made the comment.

He hadn't just guessed that Eve would climb into his bed that night.

Darius realized he had been hoping that she would.

MITCHELL NEVER WENT to his hotel. Everyone inside thought he had—and he certainly thought he was going to as well—but the second he made it to his rental's driver-side door, something heavy hit his back.

The pain was a lot to handle and, in trying to suppress it, his yell internalized. All that came out of his mouth before the woman attempted the hit again was a gasp. Not even an impressive one. The cicadas in the summer would have been louder.

Regardless of his initial reaction, the second hit was enough to make the lights go out.

When he opened his eyes again, head throbbing and stomach ready to be sick, he was in a room with a woman sitting across from him in an upholstered chair.

She was young, but confidence made her feel much older than him.

Mitchell's voice wobbled as he spoke.

"Wh-who are you?"

The woman had a gun on her lap, gloves on her hands and a clear look of annoyance on her face.

Her voice was as smooth as silk.

"Someone who was starting to get worried that I might have hit you a little too hard," she said. "The second time. The first I misjudged how tall you were. Don't worry, I have your number now."

She wasn't holding the gun, and as she crossed her legs, it moved over her thighs like a ship at sea. Mitchell couldn't help but watch the movement with a stomach that felt more than motion sickness.

The woman caught his concerned gaze and glanced down at the weapon too.

"Oh, don't worry, I'm not going to use this." She pointed down at the terrifying black metal. "I'm actually here so I don't *have* to use it at all. Because, believe me, it would be easier if I could, but, well, that's now how this plays out tonight."

"What do you mean?" Mitchell asked, voice still wobbling but at least loud enough to not be ignored. "Wh-where am I?"

He knew he was in a house, a living room, but there was nothing in his surroundings that led him to believe someone had been living in it. The furniture that was around was hidden by dust covers, the walls around them were bare, and despite the cold outside, the heater was obviously turned off and had been for a while. Even the chair he was splayed across felt rigid and cold.

However, despite the lack of life around him, Mitchell couldn't help but feel it was familiar.

The only person who knew the answer for sure smiled at him.

"I'd be less worried about where you are now and more concerned about where you're going next." That smile didn't change, but her gloved hand moved just enough that she could point down at the gun in her lap. "Because this gun?"

Pain was radiating across Mitchell's body, his stomach felt ready to empty at any moment, and neither could compete with the rising fear in his chest.

However, when the woman spoke again, every fiber of his attention attached to her words.

"It's not mine, Mr. Keys," she said. "It's yours. And I'm here to make sure you use it. So why don't we go ahead and get this job going."

Chapter Fifteen

There was a lot, she guessed, that they could have said. Eve, in bed at Darius's side, careful to keep her distance. Darius, in bed at Eve's side, polite enough to not comment on the fact that she had once again invaded his space. Yet, neither one spoke after she adjusted the blanket around her neck, trying to get warm.

And after that?

She fell asleep to silence.

It wasn't until she opened her eyes again that she finally felt the need to say something to the boy next door, now a man with a badge and a six-pack.

Mainly because, when she woke, the space Eve had been careful to give him had disappeared somewhere in the night. That chiseled upper body she had been in awe of the week before? She no longer wondered if it felt as impressive as it looked.

Eve woke up on top of it, her chin on his shoulder, her chest and stomach against his, and one leg pulled over him like she was his personal seat belt, and he wasn't going anywhere unless he unbuckled.

But it didn't seem like he had been trying to undo said seat belt during his shut-eye either. One of his hands— warm and big—was resting on the bare skin of her thigh, her shorts having shifted during sleep. The other hand and arm that weren't bandaged had wrapped around Eve to accommodate her position. She felt his fingers flex on her lower back as he also stirred from sleep.

For all the years she had slept in the same room with Darius Williams, waking up in such a position was a first.

A first that felt extremely *intimate*.

Eve might have just woken from sleep, but she was immediately and keenly aware that there was something else she could feel beneath the fabric of both of their sleeping attire. Something just south of the muscles she had been admiring.

Her face heated—her body heated—and she readied to apologize for stepping over a line she herself had drawn to give the man a boundary from her.

But something was wrong.

The hand on her thigh tightened, and her chest rumbled as Darius spoke three words, low.

"Eve, go hide."

It was the equivalent to ice water being thrown onto her face. Any vestiges of sleep, or thoughts of Darius's body, turned into alert obedience. Eve unbuckled herself from Darius and slid out of bed on swift but quiet feet. By the time she was crossing the threshold of the attached bathroom, Darius was already on his feet, heading for the gun on hand.

If it wasn't for the small light on in the bathroom behind her, Eve wouldn't have been able to see his expression.

But she could, and it let her know absolutely one thing without any context: their quiet night was about to take a turn.

Darius motioned for her to go deeper into the bathroom, a simple point-and-go. She wanted to ask what had woken him, what he had heard, what he thought was happening. Instead, she backed up and watched as he slowly turned the doorknob.

Eve held her breath. Part of her had expected to jump. But nothing, and no one came through.

That didn't stop Darius.

He raised his gun and moved into the dark hallway. Before he was out of sight, he reached back and locked the bedroom door from the inside.

Eve held out her hand to stop him. He disappeared before she could.

The small light in the bathroom did nothing to alleviate how dark the room felt after the soft click of the door closing.

Eve closed the space between it and her on bare feet. She didn't unlock the door—she didn't even touch it. Instead, she leaned close to it and listened.

Her heart was beating too loudly, racing since she had realized Darius had gone into fight mode. Her breathing, too, was off. Too fast, too distracting.

She couldn't hear anything but herself.

Eve put a hand to her chest, closed her eyes and took a deep breath.

It helped.

There was nothing at first, but then she heard a faint sound of movement.

Eve tilted her head, trying to figure out exactly where it might be coming from.

Too far away to be from the hallway bathroom or Darius's childhood bedroom. Close enough, though, that it couldn't have been the foyer or the living room.

The kitchen?

Maybe Theo had gotten up for a late-night snack? Or maybe he had risen early to go do his marathon training?

Eve realized she didn't know what time it was, just when she realized her Theo theory was most likely wrong.

The faint noise in the distance turned into something breaking. Glass shattering. A loud thump. Something scraping against hardwood.

Then, worse.

Silence.

Eve's eyes flashed opened.

Hearing a gunshot would have been more surprising.

She strained to hear something—anything.

No one spoke.

Eve reached for the doorknob.

Surely if it had been Theo that Darius had run in to they would have said something or—

Footsteps.

Eve stopped her hand midair.

They were coming down the hallway.

Maybe it was Darius.

Maybe he had come to explain what was happening.

Creak.

The floorboard outside of the door—the one Darius wouldn't have stepped on—sounded.

But Darius didn't say a word.

The doorknob, however, started to turn. It stopped at the engaged lock.

If it were Darius, this would at the very least be the first time he would say it was him. Let her know to unlock it. Called out to Eve, giving an all clear.

Instead, the silence was only broken by another twist of the doorknob.

Eve hadn't realized she was already backing up on reflex.

It made running for the window even easier when the sound of frustration went from trying the lock to someone trying to break down the door.

DARIUS PLACED HIS gun in the kitchen sink. To say he was unhappy was an understatement.

The second shooter from the steel mill, the woman who had gotten away, had now found her way back into his life.

Into his home.

And she, and the gun she had pressed against Theo's back, had backed him into a corner in the kitchen.

He hadn't yet seen the second person in his home, but he sure heard him trying with everything he had to get into the main bedroom.

"I don't know what this is, but I can tell you that he has no part in it," Darius said, aggravated. Theo's deep frown seemed to mimic the feeling. Both men were angry and trying to put a lid on that rising rage so they could all come out of this safely.

The woman wasn't taller than the boy but had angled herself to where she could see Darius clearly from his side without losing the upper hand.

Without the gun trained on him, she would have looked all but normal among them. Casually dressed, somewhere between their ages, and a pleasant-enough smile without context. Though, even without the gun in her hand, two glaring details would have eventually shattered the image.

For one thing, her lip was busted, blood dripping down her chin, and two, she was wearing black gloves.

Normal didn't seem to be on her docket.

She nodded to Theo, whose eyebrow had a nasty gash with a matching blood drip, and kept her smile tight.

"You just voluntarily put your only weapon in the kitchen

sink," she pointed out. "He might not have been a piece on the game board, but you can't argue the results of using him."

She was right.

Even as he had walked into the living room following the sounds of her and Theo's scuffle, Darius hadn't had the time or the space to go on the defense or offense. Not without risking Theo's life.

Never mind having to deal with whoever was trying to break down the bedroom door.

If the lock hadn't held, Darius wouldn't have cared if there was space or not for him to move. He would have found a way to get back to Eve come hell or high water.

But the lock and the door were holding.

Which would give Eve enough time to hide or escape.

She was, as history had shown, good at climbing in and out of windows.

"What do you want?" Darius asked. He was hoping to stall for time to figure out a plan that got everyone he cared about out of harm's way. "Why are you here?"

The woman used her free hand to wipe some of the blood away from her chin. She sighed.

"I'm running into more complications than I intended, that's why." Her hold on her weapon and aim didn't waver while she multitasked.

"Then, quit," Darius said. "Tell me who you're working for, what game they wanted you to play, and then leave. Cancel whatever deal you made, whatever contract you entered, and go."

The woman's eyes widened in obvious surprise.

She said as much.

"The honest, rule-following Detective Williams giving

me an out?" She shook her head a little. "Well, that wasn't on my bingo card for this trip, that's for sure."

Darius shrugged. He pointed at Theo.

"You holding me and my friends hostage in my house wasn't on my bingo card either," he pointed out. "Putting my gun in my sink was also something I didn't plan for. We all gain some and lose some in this."

The mystery man who had kept plowing into the bedroom door finally made progress. Before the woman could respond, the sound of splintering wood sent a new surge of adrenaline through Darius.

He didn't need to see into the hallway to know that the bedroom door was no longer hanging on its hinges.

Along with adrenaline, anger flooded his system.

He bit out a warning.

"Pull him back," he said. "Now."

The woman's smile was like the slithering of a snake. It twisted into one that indicated that she wouldn't take his order.

"I might consider this one," she said, motioning to Theo. "But everyone else needs to stay. Sorry."

She wasn't sorry, and Darius wasn't going to just stand there.

He could go backward for his gun in the sink or close the space between the woman and Theo in an attempt to disarm her. Then, he could deal with the man in his room. By then the backup that Eve had no doubt called would arrive to assist. The only variable he would have to worry about was Theo and, Theo's tensing body language probably meant he was about to try to make some kind of move to help.

Darius felt the muscles in his legs tighten in anticipation.

His fingers wanted to flex, ready to retrieve his weapon.

All he had to do now was make the first—

A body flew into view from the hallway, crashing into the woman with a loud yell and toppling her and her gun to the floor. The gun went off, but the shot embedded into the ceiling.

Darius moved quickly.

Before Theo could turn around to figure out what had happened, Darius was pushing him deeper into the kitchen.

"The sink!" he yelled.

Darius didn't wait to see if the boy understood. Instead, he joined the current fray happening in the space between the kitchen and the hallway.

And the person who had not, in fact, escaped to call for help.

Eve had attached to the woman's side like a koala. Legs wrapped around her, one arm trying to pull back the woman's neck, the other wildly flailing to try to get to the gun still in her hand.

While Darius had been surprised at her sudden appearance, their attacker looked completely taken aback by it. Her reflexes had probably kept the gun in her hand, but the rest of her didn't appear to be on the offense.

Not that she would have been able to do anything for long. Eve was too close to her—to the gun—and there was someone else in the house that, one step into the hallway, would have a clear view of Eve.

He needed the upper hand now.

Darius dropped down and grabbed the woman's wrist.

Then he broke it.

She yelled out in pain as the gun dropped from her grip and clattered to the ground.

Darius had it in his hand within a heartbeat.

Which was good because he had to pivot even more quickly.

Darius dropped his hold on the woman and switched his hand over to Eve. Timing wasn't on his side. He trained his new gun down the hallway on the bedroom door, hoping the man who had gone searching inside was slower than him.

He wasn't.

The man came out of the main bedroom, gun already up.

Darius shot the second he could. He missed but knew he would.

He was too busy yanking Eve by the shirt backward into the kitchen with all the force he had.

The sound of fabric tearing was overshadowed by the man's returning fire.

"Stop!" the woman on the ground yelled out.

The man didn't listen. Darius jumped backward into the kitchen, out of sight, while the man continued to unload his clip with no obvious regard for his partner lying in the way.

She tried to make herself flat, yelling out for the man to stop, eyes closing at each shot. Pain already etched into every syllable from her broken wrist.

Whoever the man down the hall was, he was unaffected.

Darius wasn't.

He reached down to grab the woman's leg and pulled her back with him into the kitchen. She didn't fight him, but she sure yelled.

Darius didn't join her as the man thundered into view, eyes wide and gun up.

The fact of the matter was Darius had already decided to pull the trigger the second he saw the gunman. He had been after Eve, and he had no issues about shooting at her, at his partner, and obviously no issues with killing Darius too.

This was no longer a defensive play.

He was only waiting for a kill shot.

So the nanosecond the man showed his face—sharp

lines and stubble and rage—Darius's index finger flexed, pulling the trigger with certainty.

The gun, however, had other plans.

For the first time in Darius's career, his gun jammed.

The shot that tore through the house after was deafening.

Chapter Sixteen

Eve only saw one of three things that happened all at once.

The woman lying on the floor between Darius's legs gave the man a look of such acute concern that, for that moment, it seemed she had forgotten to be angry or in pain or that fighting them might have been in her best interest.

Instead, it was worry.

She could see something that Eve, at Darius's back, couldn't see.

And that was before the shot went off.

After her gaze went from concern to blatant confusion.

Then Eve's attention split to the other two things that had happened while her focus had strayed.

A heavy thud and a slight shake of the foundation let her know that the man in the hallway had taken the single shot. At least, Eve knew it wasn't Darius. Her hands were already against his back, as if touching him let her know he was still standing. Theo had been more proactive.

He had his own gun up and was already standing at Darius's side, yelling out commands.

It confused Eve at first.

Maybe their attacker was still trying to fight? But then, why wasn't Darius moving from his spot?

Beneath her hands she could still feel the man's tension.

When it lessened, it was her sign to finally get back to reality.

Eve stepped to the side, between the two men, to size up the situation, but Darius was faster. She saw only a sliver of the attacker on the floor, blood already on the hardwood, before his hand covered her eyes.

"Don't look," he said, voice low.

Normally, she would have bucked at the command, but another voice cut her off.

"H-he's dead, isn't he?" It was a man's small voice, breaking slightly and coming from the hallway. A voice that shouldn't have been there at all.

"Mitchell?"

Mitchell made a small noise of confirmation.

"He is," Darius answered. "Theo, keep your gun on her. Mitchell, give me yours. Evelyn, turn around."

Using her full first name did the trick. Eve turned and lost the warmth of Darius's hand. The kitchen window on the far side of the room showed nothing but darkness as the rest of the people shifted around.

Darius secured Mitchell's gun, Theo secured the woman, and Mitchell appeared at Eve's side as they started making calls.

Eve would have paid more attention to it all had she not focused so completely on Mitchell when he came into view.

His face was black and blue, there was dry blood at his hairline, and there was broken and bloodied duct tape at his wrist.

"What happened?" Eve asked, hands flitting up. She didn't touch him when he flinched.

His voice was loud enough to carry to the room around them. His gaze went over Eve's shoulder. He was incredibly pale.

"She grabbed me outside when I was leaving earlier. She said I needed to come back a-and kill Detective Williams and—" Mitchell's voice broke. He took a breath. He was more quiet than before when he continued. "And you. She said that I needed to kill you."

Darius swore behind Eve.

The woman remained quiet on the floor.

Whatever fight she had had in her earlier was gone.

Mitchell shook his head.

"She said I had to be the one to do it—only me—but I said no. Never." His voice hardened. "I tried to fight her, to stop her, but that man showed up, and I guess he got me good. I woke up on the floor alone. I rushed over after and found a gun on the floor in there. I-I used it."

"My gun," Theo explained, voice as solid as Darius's had been. "I heard them breaking in and didn't have time to do anything other than defend. She got the upper hand and disarmed me. I barely had time to react." Regret laced his tone.

Darius picked up on it.

"You made enough noise to alert me," he assured him. "You gave me the time to come out and Eve enough time to escape."

Mitchell returned his gaze to Eve. His eyebrow arched.

Eve could feel Darius's unasked question hanging in the air around them.

Sirens started up in the distance. They mingled in with her sigh.

"There was no way I was leaving everyone behind." She shrugged. "I went out one bedroom window and came in through another."

It was the truth. The second she had realized the man outside of the locked bedroom door wasn't Darius was the moment Eve had gone through the main window. After that there had been no other path for her to take other than to go to her favorite window. She had climbed into Darius's childhood bedroom like a gentle breeze easing its way across a summer day. No one had heard her. Not until she had wanted to be heard.

A talking point she would get an earful about from Darius later, she was sure.

"Where was she keeping you?" he asked now.

Mitchell thumbed over his shoulder. The movement made him wince. Still, he promptly answered.

"The house next door."

"The house next door?" Eve repeated. "My house?"

Mitchell nodded.

"It's empty," Darius added.

The sirens were becoming louder. Backup was about to arrive.

It seemed to apply a new sense of pressure to the woman on the floor.

"If I were you, I'd think real quick about what happens next," she said. "You can either tell the truth and get us all killed, or you can lie and buy yourselves more time to figure out what I won't tell you. Because I guarantee you that you can't do both."

Eve couldn't see the woman still, but she easily heard the smile in her voice.

Just like she heard the anger in Darius's when he responded without hesitation.

"I suggest you shut your mouth," he said, frost on every word. "You lost any shot at bargaining with me the second you threatened *her.*"

"I now see where my fatal flaw was with this one," the

woman replied just as quickly. "I thought Miss Myers was insignificant."

She snorted.

"Judging by the look on your face, Detective, I guess we were dead wrong about that."

WINNE CAME IN CONCERNED. After glancing at Theo's beaten face, she left the kitchen angry. She took several even, quick steps back into the living room where their mystery woman was being cuffed.

Then Winnie slapped her across the face.

It was so loud it echoed.

"That's for hurting them," she exclaimed.

Her father, Price, had been the first responder on scene and was the one currently working on the woman's handcuffs. His surprise was instant and mirrored in Theo, who rushed to Winnie's side.

For a moment, Darius thought the move was unnecessary.

But then he noted her balled up hands, her widening stance and the absolute mask of anger that covered her face.

Winnie was about to attack again.

This time probably giving more than one slap.

It was a guess that proved to be correct as the young woman launched herself again at the hired hand.

Then everyone was yelling.

The woman at Price, Price at Winnie, Winnie at Theo for grabbing her, and Theo at Winnie for fighting *him* to get to the woman.

It was chaos.

And perfect for Darius.

He took a step back and quickly and quietly addressed Mitchell. Eve, at his side, listened in with a slight head tilt.

"You came over here earlier tonight because Eve and I are having an affair," Darius said, hurriedly. "You decided to end things and were attacked when leaving."

Mitchell's eyes widened.

"What?"

Darius continued, ignoring the question.

"Instead of asking for a lawyer, ask for your brother," he said. "Tell him you're afraid of me and my job in the department. Really lean into that. Got it?"

Mitchell didn't immediately answer.

Eve did it for him.

"I'll refuse to see Scott to really sell it," she added. "If they want to question me alone, I'll only ask for you."

Darius nodded.

"That'll work."

Mitchell still looked confused.

Eve patted his arm but kept her gaze on Darius.

"We've got this," she assured him.

THREE HOURS LATER and she'd proved herself right. Not only did Mitchell make a show about their alleged affair, he outright refused to answer any more questions without his brother Scott present.

Eve was the same but less flashy with it.

When she gave her statement, she did so with the sheriff and Darius at her side.

Though, the sheriff wasn't at all pleased with the situation.

He finally voiced his displeasure during a small window of quiet as everyone waited for Scott to arrive.

Liam was leaning against the wall, outside the sheriff department's bathroom, with a long face and an even longer sigh leaking out. Darius didn't miss the glance he cast around the hallways to make sure they were alone before he spoke.

"I haven't known you as long as most of the people here have, but I can confidently say that you having an affair with an almost-married woman doesn't seem to be in line with your character."

His sheriff's badge would have had a glint to it had they been out in the sun. Instead, the fluorescents made it look dull. The lack of luster wasn't reflected in the wearer. Liam had been tightly strung since seeing his son sporting blood and bruises.

He had been the only one, in fact, who hadn't reprimanded Winnie for her pointed attack on the woman who had caused it.

At any other time, Darius would have appreciated the enthusiasm.

Now he hoped to avoid its consequences.

"If it was any other woman, I wouldn't be in this situation," Darius said, telling the truth without all the details as dressings.

"But she's your childhood friend. Your former next-door neighbor."

The sheriff's words were calculated. Blunt.

Their relationship was a two-way street. Liam knew Darius was holding something back, just as Darius knew that Liam was trying to get him to admit to it.

But he couldn't.

Not yet.

So Darius stuck to the truth he could tell. The truth that might best help the sheriff understand why he was acting out of character. Or, really, why acting out of character for Eve was as in character as he could ever be.

First Darius cleared his throat.

Then he told the sheriff a story only three people in the world knew about.

The story of why, even as a boy, he would do anything for Evelyn Myers.

"When we were younger, before Eve moved, there was a boy who lived in the neighborhood who really, really didn't like me," Darius started. "Even now, two decades later, I have no idea why he hated me as much as he did. I wasn't mean to him, didn't ignore him, never fanned the flames when he still tried to bully me. He just didn't like me. Every summer he spent with his grandmother, he would find ways to peck at me. Not Eve—who, by the way, tried to fight him multiple times in my name—just me."

The heaviness of memory pressed into Darius's back.

He was uncomfortable, but he continued.

"Then one summer, something in him changed. He wasn't just some annoying kid who was annoyed by me, he was angry. And then that anger almost killed me." Liam's eyes widened a little. It was enough to verify that the man really hadn't known the story. That there hadn't been a thread of town gossip about him that Darius had managed to miss the past several years.

He was glad for it.

This was his and Eve's story. It wasn't some cheap tale to give out for some kind of shock value or as a way to break boredom.

"Before the steel mill ruled this town by itself, there was a tractor-supply company that employed a lot of the town," Darius explained. "They had two locations—the main office, and a warehouse where they stored equipment and occasionally did maintenance. The warehouse was rarely staffed unless someone actively needed to use what was inside or do a pickup. It was also two miles from my house. Which is how Jon got me there on foot and alone."

Darius shook his head, unable to avoid the anger he had at himself for being so stupid back then.

He said as much now.

"I was naive enough to believe him when he said he and Eve had found something that they wanted to show me," he continued. "The second he said Eve was there, I was already anxious that I wasn't, so I followed him into the warehouse without blinking an eye. But she wasn't there, and Jon attacked. He got the upper hand, and before I knew it, I was tied up to an old industrial rotary tiller." Darius laughed. It was in bitter disbelief, even all these years later. "He had jerry-rigged the tiller to twist the rope until it broke or until I was pulled up to the first blade."

"My God," the sheriff interrupted.

Darius understood the knee-jerk reaction. The horror, the sudden escalation of it all, had made it feel like he had been placed in a tub of ice in the moment. It wasn't until the tiller turned on and started to drag him backward that young Darius pushed his shock aside to fight against the rope.

"No matter how much he hated me, he couldn't stomach watching whatever happened next. He left when I was a foot away from the first blade." Darius shook his head a little. He could still feel the twisting panic in his stomach like it had only happened yesterday. "The rope was for industrial use, and the knot he'd tied was surprisingly effective. I couldn't untie it, and I couldn't miss that first blade, no matter how much I moved."

It had been the single most terrifying moment of his existence.

He would die alone, in a terrible way, on the floor of a

warehouse his dad and police would never think to look in, while his mother would never care to look for him at all.

The quiet son of parents who were never there, gone missing at the hands of a bully down the road.

Darius smiled.

"But I had Eve."

Warmth spread over that twisting terror in his gut.

The scariest moment of his young life held hands with one of the most profound.

"She got worried when I wasn't home, and instead of waiting around to know the reason, she went directly to Jon's house."

"How did she know he was behind it?" Liam asked. It was a genuine question, no suspicion that it might have warranted from an outsider.

Darius couldn't help but give a little laugh.

"Because she said she knew I wouldn't just leave her behind without a word," he answered. "A little kid with an overwhelming sense of confidence in her friend's loyalty to her."

"She was right."

Darius nodded.

"Jon's grandmother told her the direction we had headed in, and she took off running," he continued. "She didn't stop, not even when she passed Jon. She just kept going until she said she heard me screaming. She broke a window with a rock and found me just as the first blade was cutting into my back."

For all the serious bluster he had clung to during his career—and in most of his personal life too—Darius broke his own character and let the sheriff see something he wasn't even sure Eve had seen before.

He let Liam see him as that scared little boy on the warehouse floor.

With wide eyes, still able to fill with the absolute adoration and wonder he'd had for the little girl who had come to him covered in sweat and worry, he looked at his sheriff with every wall he'd built through the years completely down.

"Eve pulled the blade off my back just far enough to slide her hand in between and, as the blade went into her hand, she used the other one to help me untie the knot. And, when we finally got it undone and I was able to move away, do you know what the first thing she said was?" Darius didn't give him the time to answer. "She was angry she hadn't gotten there sooner."

Her hand bleeding, hair plastered to her face and neck from sweat, dirt pressed into her clothes, shards of glass still embedded in one of her shoes, and all she had been was angry at herself for not running faster.

"I never told her that, in that moment, all that fear and pain and panic I had been feeling just went away. Instead, what I felt was nothing but pride." The warmth from the moment spread through Darius, just as warm as it had as a kid. "Pride in her for being so brave and selfless. And pride in myself because, for the first time in my life, I was able to feel worthy. That something I had done had earned the unwavering love of the girl from next door."

Darius shook his head.

"That moment is the entire reason I got into law enforcement," he admitted. "She gave me a gift, and I wanted to spread that to as many people as possible to honor it. To honor her. Even after she left town and we lost touch, I never for one second forgot her. She's why I help people. She's why I try to save them. She's why, even if I can't, I'll make sure I bring whoever hurt them to justice in the end. Liam, she *is* my why."

The sheriff's expression gave nothing away.

Darius waited, knowing they were already back to the present before he asked his question.

"So the point of you telling me that story is—what? That you're not going to tell me what really is going on with you, her and the Keyses?"

Darius felt his walls rise back and settle into place again. There was no smile, no adoration in his eyes and no warmth left in his chest.

There was anger now.

"This is me telling you that there isn't anything I wouldn't do for that woman." Darius felt that anger rise. He lowered his voice, but the feeling behind it was still just as clear and loud as if he had been yelling. "And that's why, if I were you, I'd break Scott Keys before it's my turn to get to him."

Chapter Seventeen

Scott Keys was wearing his Italian leather.

That's how Eve knew that he had come to the department for blood.

"What the media will never tell you about Scott Keys is that he actually dislikes people calling him *rich*."

Eve stepped back from her spot next to the window in the break room door, no longer able to see Scott after he disappeared into a meeting room down the hall. She had only seen a sliver of him but could have spotted that outfit from space if given a glimpse.

She explained her statement to Darius and Theo, both behind her with coffees in hand.

"You can't earn respect if you pay for it, and he believes the same goes for any reputation worth having," she continued. "He wants people to see him as the charming philanthropist and not the bored trust-fund baby who likes attention. So when it comes to what he wears in public, he's always been careful to pick clothes that look nice but aren't too flashy or too easy a reminder of his inherited wealth."

Eve tapped the door, pointing in the direction of the meeting room where the sheriff was waiting.

"What he's wearing right now is more expensive than the department's salaries combined. And that's not even factoring in the shoes. Those were custom-made *in* Italy."

"Which means he's not trying to be humble right now," Darius guessed.

Eve shook her head.

"No. Right now I think he's trying to remind us that we're not on the same page as him. Not even the same book."

It had been another hour since they had arrived at the department and gone over their initial statements. The woman who had attacked them was under lock and key at the hospital, while the man who had been killed had been identified as Brae Lee, a frequent flyer at a jail two counties over for offenses that ranged from drunk-and-disorderlies to a smattering of petty thefts. He hadn't had a history of violence, but his ex-wife had been quick to let them know that in the last two years his entire personality had seemed to change.

"The man stumbled through life with nothing but cheap beer and excuses until he lost his job, our house and me," she had said on the phone, voice clear even on Speaker. "Then one day he disappears only to show up with his back straight and his pockets lined with cash. Said he found some good luck and would keep having it as long as he did some traveling and kept his mouth shut." There had been a pause. Eve had imagined the woman had shaken her head. "He never got into the details past that, and honestly, I didn't want to know. He gave me some of the worst years of my life. So I didn't want to give him anymore of my time. That was the last time I spoke to him, and I haven't had contact since."

She was sad for the loss of life and maybe a touch regretful, but she had nothing left for them to use other than the theory that whatever he had gotten into two years ago had probably led him to die in Darius's house now.

It had been enough for Darius, though. Rose and Deputy Gavin had already agreed to deep dive into the man's life to try and look for some kind of connection to the Keyses. Something Darius had officially requested in Rose's office just before they had come to the break room.

"I can't give you details, but if I were doing the looking, I'd be staring at Scott Keys and his close friend, Toby Sanderson," Darius had said. "But I'd also be a bit discreet about it too."

Eve had expected the piece of advice to get a reaction out of Rose or, at least, a question or two. Instead, she had run a hand over her pregnant belly and nodded. She had already been moving behind her desk to the computer before they could leave the room.

"He's either confident or he's trying to be intimidating," Theo said now, speaking about Scott. "Which could mean he's prepared for what happened, or he's trying to send us a warning to not involve him in it at all."

Eve nodded.

Darius shook his head.

"Or he could be here to see how much we know—or don't know—about everything that's happened."

Theo conceded.

"To be fair, at this point I'm not even sure I know what we do or don't know." He touched the butterfly bandage on his cheek. "It's been a pretty wild last week or so."

He wasn't wrong.

Coming to Seven Roads had felt like a lifetime ago. Wearing a wedding dress, standing in the middle of the road and staring at the now-grown Darius had felt even further away.

And everything that had happened since?

She'd had more questions than she had answers since arriving.

It was…frustrating, to say the least.

A frustration that they all shared, even as a silence fell over them. Eve glanced over at Darius. Her cheeks heated slightly. She wanted to talk to him in private, but she wasn't sure what to say. Or even if she should say anything at all. They were in a mess.

A mess because of a man in Italian leather.

A man with a wrath that she had yet to see come out.

Even now Eve could still feel the fear of watching Scott unleash on Mitchell in that hotel room.

The hired men and woman who had come after them so far were truly scary, but there was something about the socialite that put fire ants beneath Eve's skin.

Scott Keys didn't only have rage as a weapon. He had money.

A lot of it.

When the sheriff came to see them a few minutes later, he let them know that anger hadn't been a part of his discussion with the Keys brothers. Instead, his gaze had landed squarely on Eve.

"Scott Keys wants to see you. Both of you." Then he looked at Darius. "And I'll be frank with you here—he's not asking."

FINALLY, DARIUS MET Scott Keys.

He'd seen him, sure, nodded to him and watched as deputies had taken his statement. Darius had read the news articles too, googled him and seen enough press about him during his hospital stay to *feel* like he had met the man already.

Yet now he was in the same space. Within the same four walls.

Now he could *see* the expensive suit and shoes.

He could see the winning smile and movieworthy appearance.

And none of it mattered because all Darius cared about was Eve.

Scott wanted to hurt her.

So Darius wanted to hurt him.

But first they had to do some dancing.

Eve took the seat across from Scott. Darius didn't sit at all. He stood at her shoulder instead, gaze settling on the man in Italian leather. Scott waited in silence, eyes sharp and suit wrinkle-free. If the sheriff hadn't already given them a heads-up, Darius would have traced every detail about the man at his side to try and get more information.

He would have also showed a hint of excitement.

Before they had been attacked in his house, the plan had been to find a way to talk to Toby Sanderson and, if Darius was right, the nerve that Eve and Mitchell's secret investigation had hit before the wedding had been arranged.

So to have him already seated next to the man of the hour, wearing a suit that was notably less expensive and an expression that was also notably less calm, was like hitting the jackpot.

The man they had planned to seek out had come right to them.

And he didn't seem that enthused about it either.

Toby was fiddling with a pen between his hands as Scott finally addressed them.

"Detective Williams, I'm sure you know who I am, but who would I be if I didn't introduce myself?" Scott didn't stand. He didn't reach his hand out. He didn't make to move to at all. "My name is Scott Keys. My brother is Mitchell Keys, and I currently run the Keys Foundation. Next to me is my friend, Toby Sanderson. Typically my lawyer would be in his spot… However, he's currently a part of a homicide case file that I'm sure is still on your desk."

Scott's gaze slid down slowly to Eve.

"I also happen to be the former employer of one Miss Evelyn Myers, who I am sad to say was terminated via email before arriving at the department just now."

The silence was immediate.

It fell like a guillotine had dropped between them.

And there was a tone.

One Darius didn't like being directed at Eve.

Darius gave it right back.

"I'm Detective Williams and can confirm that, along with the people who shot me and Eve and then tried to kill us again, I am currently investigating the homicide of a Gary Whittaker." Darius put his hand on the back of Eve's chair. He wanted to seem relaxed despite the anger growing inside of him. "And while I can appreciate you keeping track of my work, I should use the same reminder to point out that my time is limited. So is this a social call, or is there a specific reason you need to talk to us?"

Toby wasn't a cool cucumber. At least not like his friend. Toby's lip curled up like he was ready to snarl at them.

Scott was more eloquent with it.

His smile was picture-polite.

"Other than my brother calling me here because he's afraid that this—" he pointed at Eve and then Darius "—new development might spell out more trouble for him, I thought it might be a good idea to come in and make a few statements to the two of you. With a witness."

Toby put the pen down.

An air of self-importance seemed to expand around him.

His restrained snarl turned into a sneer.

In any other context, Darius would have mentioned that

a good witness would be a third party with no clear side in mind.

But he was awfully curious.

Scott's stare settled on Eve again.

"To become an adulteress is already a questionable choice, but to leave a Keys at the altar at the first sign of trouble is an extremely disappointing thing," he said. "One of the reasons I hired you in the first place was because of your ability to think quickly and pivot in a high-intensity situation. Both traits I appreciated in your work over the last year. However, now I'm not so sure those truths still hold."

He paused. Not too long or too noticeably, but with enough space in between to change his expression slightly.

If Darius hadn't suspected Scott Keys of being a cruel, calculating man already, the subtle shift in his demeanor would have aroused suspicion. He wasn't outright threatening them when he spoke again, but there was an edge to every word.

"Starting next Monday there will be an investigation into your involvement with the Keys Foundation, the personal lives of the Keys family, and any and all connections to our beloved late Gary Whittaker." Scott cut a quick look to Darius. "Since we aren't sure where the law enforcement priorities lie, we will make sure that you *will* answer for any wrongdoings that you have committed for your own personal gain. And then you will pay for everything you have done."

The last statement hit hard.

Darius's body reacted faster than his brain.

His fist balled into the fabric of the chair back, rage no longer rising but instead crashing across his entirety.

Scott was back to looking at him again. He must have seen the change.

A whisper of a smile seemed to cross the rich man's lips.

Not only had he just clearly threatened Eve, he'd come into Darius's domain to do it.

And not only that—he'd done it in front of Darius too.

It was nothing short of infuriating.

It was also about to earn Darius's not-so-composed wrath.

He opened his mouth to say something—he wasn't exactly sure what—when another voice unexpectedly joined the chat.

"Fair enough." Eve's voice wasn't small or weak. It was loud and steady. She waited for the men across the table from her to focus before she continued.

Which is how Darius was able to read the absolute surprise in them when she spoke again.

"And when they investigate, they'll find my investigation into you."

Instead of looking at Scott, Darius could tell by the turn of her head that Eve was staring right at Toby.

His eyes widened. He opened and closed his mouth like a fish out of water for a moment.

"Me? What do you mean investigation into me? Investigation into what?"

She shrugged.

"Oh, you know, just the whole you visiting small towns before some kind of calamity happens, only to then pave the way for our White Knight here to ride in and save the day. At first I wondered if it was just a coincidence—your bad luck—but then I saw the pattern and understood that you're either one of two things, Mr. Sanderson."

Eve tapped the table's top between them.

"You're either a man who brings the plague, or you're the man who tells others to bring it. Then, after it spreads, you get to sit back and watch as your best friend, with all his resources and money, cures what you helped infect."

Toby shook his head, anger and shock deepening his frown.

"That's *ridiculous*," he exclaimed. "You think *I* have been—what?—sabotaging random towns through the years? That sounds like a bad plot to a bad movie. Can you believe this, Scott?"

The man in question hadn't moved a muscle.

His face was like stone.

As he answered, his words were just as hard.

"That's quite the accusation there, Miss Myers," he said. "If I had known you had such an imagination, I wouldn't have wasted your talents by simply hiring you as my assistant."

Most people might have heard the cold in his words—the edge that was there too—and decided against continuing to push.

But most people weren't Eve.

She pushed her chair back and stood.

Compared to the White Knight of Small-town Living, the woman dressed in plain jeans and a fuzzy sweater seemed to suddenly tower over them all.

It only added to the sudden change in demeanor when she lightly laughed.

"What can I say? You were right about me, Scott. It turns out I *am* good at thinking on my feet. That's how I found your flight logs, Toby. All of them."

Without waiting for a reaction, Eve turned and walked right out of the meeting room.

It gave Darius full view of the men sitting across the table from him.

Toby was confused, quiet with it too. The pen he had been fiddling with lay forgotten beneath his hands.

Scott was also quiet.

But his stare was burrowing a hole into Darius.

Whatever the White Knight of Small-town Living was feeling…it wasn't good.

Chapter Eighteen

There was a lot that was said in the department after that. Eve, thankfully, heard little to none of it while sitting in Darius's office with Winnie. The younger woman shared a bag of cookies with her while Theo, his father the sheriff, Winnie's father the deputy, and Darius were going room to room, doing who knew what.

All Eve did know was that she was in deep trouble no matter how she looked at what she had done.

Sometime within their stay inside of Darius's office, Eve let out a sigh that was loud, long and filled with defeat.

"I'm doomed," she said. "Big doomed. Doomed bad. Badly doomed. The worst doomed."

Winnie had been poring over information on her laptop, forgotten cookie hovering over the trackpad while she did so.

At this stream of exclamations, she looked up.

"I've seen this department come together and protect each other before, even against some pretty scary odds. No matter what Mr. Keys decides to do, they won't let anything happen to you or Mitchell."

Eve lolled her head to the side to look at the girl head on.

"I wasn't talking about this business with Scott, Toby and the hired hitpeople."

It took Winnie a second, but she finally clued in. A small smile turned up the corner of her lips.

"You're afraid of Detective Williams," she clarified. "Because you basically told the bad guys that you knew they were bad and exactly what evidence you had to prove it."

Eve dropped her head down and huffed.

"It wasn't like I was planning to do it," she defended. "It just kind of came out."

That was as true as a truth could be. Sitting there across from Scott with his fancy shoes and Toby with his nonchalant attitude had been grating. But not for the reasons it should have been.

Scott had requested to talk to her *and* Darius to threaten them. To threaten her. To fire her and make a show of it.

And he'd brought Toby to do it.

That grating against her nerves had been a noise that had transformed into absolute quiet once Eve had realized this might be her only chance to play their own hand.

They hadn't been certain that the flight records of Toby's private jet had been the reason for Scott pushing for the wedding, for Gary's murder or for the subsequent attacks.

So Eve had gambled with the piece of potential evidence.

Or, really, she had used it as bait.

Bait that had forced Darius to make his own moves.

He had put her in his office without an explanation of what he was about to do, only that she and Winnie needed to wait.

It felt like waiting outside of the principal's office in school.

She was definitely going to get a talking-to about her behavior.

Eve pushed herself forward in the roller chair, tucking

her legs up against her chest as she did so. Her shoulder hurt a little, but she had more pressing things to worry about.

"I wanted to help us skip to the end of this thing," she said. "It feels like months since Gary's body was found. And after last night, I can't stand waiting for the other shoe to drop on us. I'd rather throw my own shoe first to see what happens."

"I understand why you did it," she said. "Last night was terrifying, and I wasn't even there."

Winnie's tone was soft and caring, a far cry from how the young woman had yelled at their attacker at Darius's house. Theo's attacker. She had only fully settled down once she was sitting next to Theo after the paramedics had given him the okay.

Though, if Eve were a betting woman she would put money on the fact that Winnie's cute and gentle appearance could transform into feral at any moment. A kind of feral that would probably put the men around them to shame.

It's one reason why Eve liked Winnie so much. She felt a kinship there.

She also was starting to be so fond of Winnie for the simple fact that both she and Theo genuinely seemed to care about Darius. Even though both of their parents worked at the department, they had stayed in proximity to their detective. Theo had left them in the office as Darius's shadow earlier. Eve had no doubt he would return with the ready-to-scold-her detective too.

"Do you think he'll really be mad at me for showing my hand to Scott and maybe messing up the investigation?" Eve paused midspin to ask. If it had been Theo, he would have probably just nodded. Instead, Winnie was thoughtful with her answer.

"I think he'll raise his voice and huff at you, but I don't

think he's mad." She put the cookie in her hand down and finally closed her laptop. "I think he's just worried, you know? And not because of the investigation. He cares about you, and you just spit in the face of the monster he's trying to catch. No matter how good a detective he is, he can't predict the future. He knows that, which means he knows that he'll never be able to one-hundred-percent keep you from getting hurt. That plus the fact that both of you have already been shot probably isn't helping his frustration."

Eve let her mouth hang open a little. She hadn't expected an in-depth opinion. One that, after her accidental eavesdropping earlier, made a slow blush slid up to her cheeks.

She tried to play the feeling off.

"You make it sound like I'm more important to him than I am," Eve said. "I haven't even seen the man in over twenty years."

Winnie's smile was small and warm. Her next question caught Eve off guard.

"Have you had any serious boyfriends in those twenty-something years?"

Eve was further thrown off by how immediate her *no* was.

"I mean, there was really no time for it when I was younger," she tacked on. "I was taking care of my dad, and then I was working to pay off our debt. Then I was trying to find my place in the world, and well, I didn't have much space to do anything."

"So you've never dated anyone? Ever?"

There was no pressure or harshness in Winnie's questions. Just a genuine curiosity.

It made Eve pause a little to think about the best way to phrase her answer.

"No, I did date some," she admitted. "Though, I'm not

sure any of it counts. Most were double dates from coworkers where they dragged me along, while others were just
casual meetups or as a result of bumping into someone. I
tried a dating app once, went to the movies and had a nice
meal, but it didn't work out. None of them ever worked out."

Winnie's gaze was expectant.

With a small sigh of defeat, Eve smiled as she continued.

"As silly as it sounds, as *pathetic* as it sounds, I think a
part of me just kept looking for the boy next door."

"Detective Williams," Winnie expounded.

Eve nodded.

"Before I left, we were best friends with just a pure, innocent friendship. And yet I think Darius somehow became
my standard for everything." It was true, Eve realized. Now
more than ever. Sure, she'd had her first kiss. Her first time.
Her first boyfriend in name and then her first breakup. She
had experienced different dates and men and had tried her
best to…care. But none of them had stuck. Not like the boy
next door had. "I had a coworker who was a little too in-
vested in my lack of love life and would try every day to
sell me on the ideal of true love and soul mates. One day
she was really, really insistent on me putting myself out
there so I'd find a half."

"Find a half," Winnie repeated.

"Everyone is out there in the world looking for their
other half, so when they find them they can finally feel
whole," Eve said. "She said no matter how hard I was fak-
ing it, no one can be happy as a half."

Eve raised her hand to stop whatever feelings Winnie
might have had about that.

"I don't think that's true," Eve added quickly. "I think
people can be whole all by themselves, and if they want to

be with someone, that someone can add on to their lives and be just as meaningful—"

Winnie was quick. "But?" she ventured.

Eve knew she should have felt embarrassed or shy or something at what she said next. She didn't, though.

"Since the days when Darius let me in through his bedroom window as kids, I've never been able to move on from him." No heat ran up her neck or pooled in her cheeks. No warmth surrounded her heart or flooded her belly. She felt completely unchanged. What she was saying was just a fact. "And I know it's wild to say that some boy I knew as a kid—the same boy I didn't see for over twenty years—completely changed me, but he did. I think that's why I've never really settled, at least when it comes to relationships. Part of me just..."

Eve tilted her head to side, as if movement would make it easier to find the right words.

She wasn't sure if it worked.

She simply said what she now knew as true.

"Part of me just never forgot that window. Never forgot the boy sitting inside that room." Eve ran a thumb across the side of her hand. The one she had gotten at the warehouse all those years ago. Their first matching scar. She lowered her voice, tired for the woman who had gone on those dates, trying to figure out why she couldn't make her heart move at all. Trying to find her other half but eventually giving up when she couldn't.

Now Eve understood why it had never worked.

Why it never would.

It was such a jolting revelation, and yet it didn't really feel like anything all that new.

Eve looked at Winnie and told her straight and true.

"I've never been able to find my other half out there because I've never been a half myself. Not since I met Darius. Without trying to, without meaning to, and I guess without me realizing it either, *he* made me whole."

That was the long and short of it.

The damn ridiculous truth.

Eve had grown up loving Darius Williams without reservation, without any doubt and without knowing it. And after seeing him again on the county road, her wearing a wedding dress and him wearing a badge, that love had stretched its legs and decided to walk somewhere it hadn't yet walked before.

"I guess I'm in love with him," Eve admitted. She nodded once to herself to confirm it. "And I suppose I always have been. Maybe that's why I never noticed. Like one day you open your closet and all your clothes are blue. You never realized it was your favorite color, but the evidence sure is clear once you look close enough."

Eve watched as the younger girl's gaze widened.

She couldn't help but laugh a little.

"Sorry, I didn't mean to have such a personal epiphany right in front of you," she said. "Probably not what you expected to hear."

Despite the potential awkwardness, Winnie collected herself well. She showed a smile that felt as genuine as every smile Eve had seen the girl make since they had met.

"I'll take a beautiful epiphany over drama-filled gossip any day, so don't worry. I'm actually grateful you told me. I feel honored." Her smile grew until her eyes wrinkled a little. Eve mimicked the growth. Just as she let it drop as Winnie's started to fade.

"Are you going to tell Darius?" she asked.

"Tell him what? That he's the only person I think I've ever fully and completely loved?" Eve snorted. "After the trouble I brought him—brought you and this town—I don't think I have the right to flood the waters any more than I already have. Not after I left him alone here."

The last part Eve hadn't meant to say. Truly, it had been the only part of her feelings she had hoped to keep close to her chest.

Because it was guilt.

Winnie's eyebrow arched high.

"You mean when you went to Texas with your dad to take care of him? It's not exactly like you had a choice."

That guilt in Eve soured the warmth she had finally been able to identify in her chest.

"Then, what was my excuse for the last twenty years?" she asked. "Why did I only come back when there was trouble?"

It wasn't a question that was meant to be answered. Not by Winnie and certainly not by Eve. There was no answer that would ever be enough in her opinion.

She had made a promise to Darius's mother that he was hers. For life.

Then she'd disappeared from his for twenty years.

Loving Darius Williams was one thing.

Asking him to love her back was another.

And Eve just couldn't do that to him.

Winnie opened her mouth, probably readying to encourage her, if Eve had to guess, but the attempt was cut off by a knock against the doorframe.

Eve swiveled in her chair to see Theo and his laptop bag swung over his shoulder. He shared a quick look between them before pointing in the direction of the front of the department.

"Everything has been taken care of for now, which means it's time for us to head home," he announced.

Eve stood at once, the chair rolling back behind her and hitting the desk with a little too much force.

"Is there any more news? What do we do when we get there? What happens next?"

Eve and her confession were replaced by Eve and her anxiousness to be done with Scott Keys and his potential retaliation.

Theo put his hands up in self-defense against the interrogative onslaught, but it was Darius who spoke next. He came into view with his eyes down on the phone in his hand.

"What happens next is us going to get some sleep, since none of us got anything worth anything last night," he said.

"Wait. You can't just go back to your house," Winnie pointed out. "What if another hired killer or someone else shows up to attack you? Especially now that they know about the flight records?"

Winnie the Feral Fighter of Theo-attackers was coming back up to the surface. Her words were no longer gentle and warm. Theo's eyes went to her at the change. It might have been Eve's imagination, but it almost seemed like his cheeks reddened a little at it.

Darius didn't look up from his phone as he answered.

"Everyone has a place to go that should be safe. Theo is going with you back to your dad's place, Mitchell is going with Deputy Gavin to his sister's place since she's out of town for a while, and Eve and I are going to my second house. Since only two people know about it, it's the best option for now."

"Your second house? You have a *second* house?"

Eve tilted her head to the side, once again physically moving like the act would shake an answer loose before he could give one.

Which would have been nice considering how slow it felt for Darius to answer her with a nod.

Those eyes—dark and familiar—met hers a moment later.

"If you want to find out, follow me and see."

Eve didn't need more than that. She grabbed her bag, let Winnie out into the hallway first and paused as Darius reached around her to turn off the office light. Then she followed him without hesitation out into the cold midday air.

It wasn't until they were sitting in Darius's truck that Eve spoke again.

"What if I really did put a larger target on myself?" she asked. "Are you sure that it wouldn't be safer for everyone if I stayed at the department?"

Darius snorted as he put the truck in gear.

"We'll never know, so there's no point in wondering."

Eve gave him another questioning look.

"What do you mean, we'll never know? I could stay and we could—"

Darius was quick this time. He cut her off before she had a chance to continue.

"We'll never know because leaving you isn't an option." Those dark eyes were back on her. She could see herself reflected in him as he leaned in close.

"Just so we're clear. From now until the end, I'm going to be by your side, Evelyn Myers. So I suggest you get used to it."

Chapter Nineteen

"You bought my house."

Eve was standing in the middle of the living room, bag already dropped on the floor next to her.

Darius, having finished checking all the rooms to make sure they were clear again, scooped the bag back up. He nodded.

"The man who was using it as a rental retired and went to Florida. He sold it to me at a good price, and I've been working here and there on it when I have the time ever since."

Eve's eyes and mouth were both wide.

Darius left her to her surprise and backtracked to the first room on the left.

He heard her footfalls hurrying behind him but didn't stop until he was inside the bedroom and in front of its closet. He unzipped her duffel bag before reaching for some hangers that were plastic-wrapped in the corner.

His shoulder pulled a little at the movement, but he was more interested in the woman currently standing behind him.

Darius had never once felt weird about buying the house next door. In fact, it had seemed a must for him the second he had seen the For Sale sign. However, he also hadn't expected the girl who used to live in it to come back and find out.

At least, not the way she had.

Now he tried to look at her reaction while busying his hands with her clothes.

"You bought my house and…you kept my room." She pointed to the old bed frame and then the nightstand between it and the wall. "That's mine. I mean, it *was* mine. Dad built it for me, but we didn't have the room to take it in the move. We put it by the side of the road, right?"

Eve had never been a particularly sentimental girl when it came to material things, but on that day right before they moved, Darius had seen her cry. When she had gone to the store with her dad later that afternoon, Darius had hurried to grab the piece of furniture before squirreling it away in their shed. Kid Darius didn't know what he would do with it, but he knew he didn't like seeing her cry over it.

"The previous owner kept the frame, and I kept the nightstand." Darius shrugged. "Refurbishing them saved me money in the long run. You can't argue with saving money, right?"

Eve's footsteps were moving farther away. Darius took a folded shirt from her bag and placed it on the first hanger. He glanced over his shoulder at her as he hung it up.

She had her hand placed on the nightstand's top.

"You kept this to save money but bought my house? Sounds like you lost money to me."

Darius found the second folded shirt. It was blue and worn. A T-shirt with a logo that had long since faded. He could smell the fabric softener on it.

It was nice.

"After buying *my* house, buying this one seemed like a good investment," he defended. "It is, as you might have noticed, right next door after all. Not only a good investment but an easy one to manage, since all I have to do to see it is look out of the window."

He put the shirt on the hanger and then went back to the duffel for another. There were two pairs of pants, all bunched-up together. Darius took both pairs out. He walked them over to the dresser against the wall. He wasn't going to point out that it was *his* childhood dresser.

Eve might not have been sentimental about these things, but Darius had surprised himself with his own soft spot for them. He had seen her old nightstand and couldn't help but feel like it needed something to match it.

What better piece of furniture than something from his childhood too?

"And no one knows you own it? Mitchell being held here was a coincidence?" Eve was standing in front of the window. The curtains over it were drawn save for a sliver between. The world outside had grown hazy and dark from an overcast sky. Still, she stood in the small strand of light and gazed out.

Darius finished putting her pants away before he answered, careful with his words.

"Mitchell being taken here, if I had to guess, was an act of opportunity since this place has been empty," he said. "Other than the sheriff and his friend who was the Realtor before he moved, the purchase didn't get broadcasted like other news seems to around here. The fact that Seven Roads has been through a lot through the last few years helped too, I'm sure." He laughed a little. "Compared to the rest of town, I've been the least interesting one here. If the gossip mill has found out, no one has shared the info. Who cares if the grumpy detective buys an empty house?"

Darius's attention had already slipped back to the duffel he had placed on top of the dresser. The next items he could see inside were small, black and cotton. He was already wondering if it was right for him to put them away when he heard the floor squeak a little behind him.

Two arms wrapped around his back. Eve fastened her hands at his chest to close the circuit.

Then all he felt was warmth.

The warmth of Eve as she burrowed into his back and flattened her cheek against his shoulder blade.

Her voice was small.

"I care."

Silence overlapped the two simple words. One wave coming to shore before returning to the sea. Strong, natural and then gone.

Darius took a moment to enjoy the wave before it crashed.

He put his hand over hers.

The heat came on in the living room, its buzz soft but noticeable.

Darius's phone made noise next, also soft but noticeable.

He patted her hand. She let him go.

The caller was Rose. He turned to Eve before answering the phone.

"I know you're worried about being found here, but I promise you we're safe now," he said. "This place is ours."

He meant to say it was their secret.

He didn't amend his words, though.

Instead, Darius watched as Eve nodded, a small frown at odds with the cuteness of her fuzzy little sweater.

"I trust you," she said.

Darius nodded in turn.

He excused himself to the living room, past the spot where Mitchell had been held the night before, past the living room window that looked out at his house, and answered the phone.

He listened to every word Rose said next, but part of him was still in the bedroom, Eve pressed against him in the quiet.

THERE WAS AN upset at the hospital as the afternoon rolled around. Apparently, the woman who was hired to come after them was tougher than she looked. After the surgery she'd had on the wrist that Darius had broken, she had tried to escape. Not only had she tried to do so without a weapon but also while still coming down off anesthesia.

The deputy assigned to her had been able to disable her before she could get on the elevator.

"If she hadn't tried so hard to kill us, I would be impressed," Eve decided, toothbrush in hand.

The afternoon haze had officially dissolved into the night, and Darius had finally called it quits. No more phone calls, no more researching, no more compulsively checking the security cameras on the house or the one next door.

Now it was just the two of them getting ready for bed.

"And for that same reason, I'm astounded that we still have no idea who she is," he said, putting his own toothbrush back into its holder.

While Darius had spent most of the day on the phone, Eve had spent some of her time walking the same floors she had as a little girl.

Much like his own childhood home, Darius had changed everything save a few pieces of the familiar. The tired carpet had been updated to hardwood. The guest bathroom had been painted and the hardware updated. The kitchen cabinets had been replaced and a fairly new refrigerator stood where their less-than-aesthetically pleasing former one had stood. The room that had once belonged to her father had a new bedroom suite, along with curtains that were as subtle as the new wall color. There were still some signs that the en suite was being updated, but even still nothing in it fit the memory Eve had of the room.

It was only the first bedroom on the left that she recognized with one foot in the past and one in the present.

And Eve had no idea how to feel about any of it.

Darius had bought her home and saved parts of her childhood.

What did that mean?

Did he still feel like he owed her for what had happened at the warehouse when they were kids? Had some kind of misguided guilt led him to make such a drastic decision?

Or was it really about an easy investment?

Eve huffed now at the reflection in the bathroom's mirror.

Darius must have thought it had to do with their current predicament. He walked past her to the bedroom.

"Don't worry," he said, oblivious to the almost-constant series of questions she had been listening to on repeat in her head since the discovery. "She might be good, but I'm better. We'll figure out who she is."

Eve trailed behind him, nodding.

She followed him into the guest bedroom, still nodding.

When he pulled back the covers and slid into the bed, she stopped.

Her eyebrow arched high. He caught the confusion and returned a small eye roll.

"I figured it would save you some time and energy by starting out in the same bed instead of having you creep around later." He grabbed the covers next to him and pulled them away from the sheets. "You can go ahead and just start at the end."

He was right, of course.

There had been no way—great love epiphany or not—that Eve was going to sleep a wink without having Darius beside her. She hadn't even napped earlier despite his insistence.

Yet she hadn't actually thought about what that meant until now. Or, really, how she felt about it now that she *had* finally realized that her love for the man was no longer just loyalty or friendship. Instead it was her—a woman very much aware of how that boy had grown up well—about to slide in next to him in bed wearing her little PJ set and no makeup, and swimming in a lot of feelings.

Darius was back to looking at his phone, texting someone. Eve used the distraction to hurry to her place. She pulled the covers up to her chin. Darius continued to go through his phone.

Minutes went by, and slowly the foreign awkwardness Eve was feeling fell away. She wiggled her toes under the covers and stared at the ceiling.

The same old popcorn treatment with light from the nightstand lamp discoloring it to an off-white. She tried to remember the last time she had been in the same room. The night before the move, she had stayed in Darius's. Him on the floor, her lying on the side of his bed, hand draped over to hold his blanket.

Pure friendship. Pure loyalty. Pure love.

That was enough for her.

She could grow old with it. With him.

Like this.

In the silence.

In the same room.

In love, but knowing it wasn't her place to expect him to want anything more.

Eve let out a small breath and rolled onto her side. She reached out and turned her lamp off.

A few minutes later Darius turned his off too.

Eve could still make out the window a few feet away.

Muscle memory nearly made her move.

There was no point climbing out tonight when the boy next door was already there.

Eve closed her eyes.

And then an arm wrapped around her.

Beneath the sheets, Darius's bare arm slid across her hip and hooked up between her breasts. His hand balled into a fist, twisting her shirt in his grasp. It was a gentle hold that kept her steady as the rest of him moved into place. Every curve of her was met by every curve of him. His chest to her back, his hip to her hip, his knees to the backs of hers, his forehead to her hair.

No space was left between them.

Even as he spoke, the only place his words had to go were into the back of her neck.

"I never blamed you for leaving, Eve."

His words rumbled through his chest and into her back.

"But you never looked for me either," she pointed out.

"When you didn't reach out, I thought you were happy. I didn't want to mess that up."

Eve smiled.

"And I thought you were happy and didn't want to mess it up either," she countered. "Now look at me. I came back with nothing but baggage. Messy, complicated baggage."

Her eyes felt hot.

Guilt, anger, frustration, longing.

Years of stress and listlessness.

A broken ship on the sea, hoping to see a storm but instead lost in an endless boring calm.

A life that had been lived on autopilot.

And then suddenly seeing a familiar island on the horizon.

But it had been too long.

The landscape had changed.

It was no longer an island deserted.

There were other people and boats and stories that she had never been a part of.

Time hadn't stopped for a moment since Eve had left Seven Roads, and while she had grown up, Darius had too.

And it killed Eve so badly that she finally admitted it out loud.

"I missed everything," she managed, voice breaking. "Life passed me by and…and everyone else went with it."

Eve knew she wasn't making sense. Or maybe she was being too dramatic. But she couldn't help it.

Even as Darius slowly turned her over, careful of their injuries, and lay on his side while staring down at her, Eve couldn't help but cry.

His smile was barely visible in the light from the small opening from the curtains.

He took the side of her face into his hand and ran his thumb across her cheek, wiping away the few tears that were still there.

"Evie, I bought an entire house for one window. What part of that makes you think I was ever planning on moving on without you?"

It wasn't her first kiss.

It wasn't her second or third. Heck, it wasn't even her tenth.

But when Darius lowered his lips to hers, Eve felt like the world around them simply stopped.

He was warm; he was gentle. His tongue parted her lips

and mingled with hers as Eve accepted the advance. The hand on the side of her face slid behind her neck as the tips of his fingers tangled into her hair.

Eve went with the movement and angled her chin higher.

The new position made it easier for their kiss to deepen.

The rest of the world around them might have felt like it stopped, but Eve sure didn't hesitate for a moment.

Darius might have been focusing on the kiss, but Eve had already skipped ahead.

She pulled him down onto her with hungry hands and used her legs to get the rest of him. It gave him two options: change his hold on her to accommodate a more intimate hold, or keep the kiss without giving in.

Bless him, Darius chose the former.

He let her neck go and broke their kiss long enough to rock backward.

Eve went with him.

And apparently it humored him.

"What?" she asked, barely able to catch her breath. She was now the one looking down at him. Still, she heard the smile in his voice before she saw it.

His hand flattened against her thigh at his side.

"You went from crying to straddling really quick is all," he said. "It's almost like you've really been wanting this."

Eve huffed.

"You're one to talk about really wanting this." She adjusted herself slightly on his lap. There was a notable hardness right beneath her. Her rubbing against it nearly made her lose her composure. She guessed it was a mutual struggle. Eve heard his breath catch just enough to know that he was absolutely affected by her.

"If you have a problem with me doing this, I can always just leave," she offered when he didn't immediately respond.

That threat surely did a number on the man beneath her.

The hand on her thigh joined the other as they both slid up her legs, beneath her PJ shorts and underneath her panties. He grabbed her bare hips and pulled down, applying pressure exactly on the part of him that couldn't lie about the pleasure he felt with her being on him.

This time, Eve was the one to make a little gasp.

"Where you go, I go," he said. "If you want to leave, I won't stop you. *But...*"

He bucked up against her, not enough to move her off, but enough to let her feel just how hard he wanted her.

"But...?" she asked, this time absolutely breathless.

Darius's voice also changed.

Now he was gravel and grit.

"*But* let's save us both some trouble and just spend the night in this room."

It wasn't a question, and even if it had been, Eve wouldn't have needed to give an answer.

They both knew neither one of them were leaving.

Not each other.

Not the room.

And certainly not the bed.

Chapter Twenty

Lana's world flipped upside down as the cruiser was driven off the road. One second she was strapped into the back, the next her hair and arms were dangling downward to the roof of the car.

Her first instinct was to check on her wrist, fresh from surgery, and the sling that had come loose.

The next was to escape.

She unbuckled her seat belt and thudded against the roof of the car. One of the windows had blown out, and broken glass pressed against the scrubs she had been given after her surgery. If the glass had cut into her clothes and skin, she still wouldn't have slowed. Where there was a will, there was a way, and now she could see that one of the windows that was no longer in one piece just so happened to be one she could reach.

A groan sounded from the front. One of the two deputies meant to escort her to the sheriff's department was obviously still alive.

But she wasn't going to check on him.

Lana scrambled through the pain, and the window, until her good palm felt dead grass and dirt. A line of trees wasn't too far from her. Once she got among the trees, even hurt she could outrun law enforcement.

After that?

She could disappear again.

This time, she wouldn't come back.

This time—

"I suggest you don't run just yet."

A man's voice interrupted her evolving plan. It was so even and calm that her curiosity paused her flight response.

Lana turned to see if he looked as composed as he sounded, standing at the top of road's shoulder. He wasn't too young and he wasn't too old and wore what she imagined someone would wear to a business interview. Khakis, a button-up and a thin jacket with a common logo on its chest. She had never seen him before, but he obviously knew who she was.

He pointed back to the road. The SUV that had created their crash was waiting, passenger-side door open.

"There's a new job," he said.

Lana's head swam a little as got to her feet. She made sure not to show the discomfort.

"Who are you?" she asked.

The man laughed.

He might have looked plain, but something about him made Lana suppress a shiver.

"I'm plan B."

THE SMALL SLIVER of light from the window the night before was no longer nostalgic or cute. It was annoying.

Eve swatted at the nuisance before rolling over to bury her face into the covers.

It took a few beats to realize there wasn't a man where he used to be.

Suddenly, Eve was wide awake.

She rolled onto her back and stared wide-eyed at the ceiling.

The night before had never been on a list of possibilities for Eve. And never had she thought that sharing a bed with Darius would lead to anything other than talking. Maybe an accidental cuddle after she had fallen asleep.

Not a kiss.

Not everything that had followed.

Warmth went from below her waist right up to her cheeks.

And everything certainly had happened.

Eve placed her hands on her face and did a little wiggle. She wasn't embarrassed, but she wasn't going to pretend that she was calm either.

She had already loved every inch of Darius before their time together, but now? Now she'd seen and touched most of those inches. How could they come back from that?

Did they come back from that?

Or were they not something new?

Were they together?

Or had the familiar just been the only thing they could cling to with all the chaos around them?

Eve slid her hands down her face, sighing once her lips were clear.

After their time together the night before, they hadn't talked much. At least not about what had changed between them, not about their relationship, their futures. They had showered, gotten back into bed and fallen asleep quickly.

They hadn't gotten down to the fine print of their new arrangement.

But he had to care about her, right?

Eve flung the covers off and hurried out of bed. A soreness south of her waistline reminded her that she definitely hadn't been dreaming about what they had done either.

How Darius reacted to her now would surely give her an idea of what he was thinking. If he didn't say a word about it, then she wouldn't either. If he declared his love for her? She would already be yelling hers at him. If he admitted it was nothing but a safe place to rest with someone he knew wouldn't give him grief after? Well, she would probably go cry in the bathroom when he wasn't looking.

Either way, Eve decided that it was now or never.

She *had* to have some kind of answer.

She threw her hair up high, took her jeans from the dresser and pulled on an old shirt. On reflex she patted her back pocket once she was dressed. Her phone was, of course, not there.

Remembering where her cell had been plugged in the night before, Eve turned to the nightstand, and something caught her eye at the window.

Her blood turned to ice.

The gap between the curtains was filled with a face.

Someone was looking in.

A woman.

Eve would later wonder if everything would have gone differently had she not moved. If she had screamed or called out for Darius. If she had run from the room, never once looking back.

Would things have gone better?

But in the moment, Eve didn't yell. She didn't run. She didn't scream.

Instead, she hesitated.

That's the only reason she saw the woman put her hand up to the window. And that's the only reason she noticed the writing scrawled across her palm.

Save them.

It was the woman from the steel mill. The one who had broken into the same house the day before. Eve could see the sling was still on. She could also see that the woman wasn't holding a weapon.

There was blood, though, along her hairline and dripping down the side of her face.

Maybe that was why Eve went to the window and, against all her better judgment, slid the curtains to the side.

When the woman made no immediate move to attack or show aggression, Eve took her lack of judgment even further.

She unlocked the window and slid it up a few inches. Just enough to hear her.

The woman didn't waste any time.

"A man is in your living room threatening to kill Theo Weaver, Winnie Collins, and Deputy Collins to get your detective to leave the house with him," she rushed. "He wants Detective Williams to lure *you* out, but if he finds out you're here, then he'll kill the detective without a second thought."

Like she had timed it perfectly, there was a commotion coming from the front of the house. Yelling. But no shots.

Yet.

Eve glanced at her phone.

The woman hurried on.

"They can track phones, but they can't track me," she said. "Leave with me now, and you can save them all later." The commotion from the other side of the house became louder. The woman might have been bleeding, hurt and pale, but her words were steady, her eyes clear. But that didn't mean Eve could believe her.

"Why would you help me?" she asked. "You've attacked us before."

Despite the intense situation, the woman actually rolled her eyes.

"I'm breaking my contract, and the only way to not get killed is to help you guys not get killed."

Eve's adrenaline spiked as something in the other room shattered.

Her heart squeezed.

"Why?" she had to ask once more.

The woman was nothing but serious when she answered again.

"Because when enough men keeping telling you to kill a woman, it's always a good rule of thumb to reevaluate. Now, come on so we can outsmart those idiots." The woman stepped to the side, angling her body away from the house. She looked seconds away from running.

Not attacking.

All concerns about Eve's relationship with Darius disappeared.

With no real evidence, Eve decided she believed the woman completely.

So much so that she took her cell phone off the nightstand, hid it under the blanket on the bed and grabbed her coat.

She was out the window and running before the door to the bedroom even opened.

THE WINDOW WAS OPEN, and Eve was gone.

Good girl, Darius thought, gun to his back, and the man holding it laughing behind him. *Now, stay gone this time.*

"I guess some things just don't change," the man said. "If there's a window, Eve surely will find a way through it."

The man must have shrugged. The gun moved against him slightly.

"I suppose I should have been quieter, though," he continued. "But you know what they say about hindsight. Twenty-twenty and all that."

Darius was hurting. Not only had the man gotten inside the house and beaten him good, Darius had let it happen. All because of the picture the man had showed him on his phone.

A picture of Winnie and her father, tied up and bloody somewhere nondescript.

It had been the master key to every space in both of Darius's houses.

A master key that would have broken, had Eve not fled through the bedroom window.

Darius was glad for her quick thinking so she was out of danger.

But also because of who the man was.

This time, Darius had recognized his attacker.

This time, he knew the danger had pushed them all to the brink.

"I should have kept better track of you," Darius bit out, turning to face the fourth gunman of the week. "Last I heard, you were incarcerated in Tennessee."

Jon Decanter had aged, and not just in the simplest of terms. Time had been unkind to him, taking a boy who had been Darius's age and making him a man who appeared older, more worn and grizzled. His clothes gave him the appearance of a PTO dad, but the scars along his jaw and arms spoke to a different kind of lifestyle.

His gaze, however, hadn't changed.

Hate rested there.

Angry and all too familiar.

"You track me?" Jon laughed again, the sound chilling. "Like little Evie would let you do that. After what she did, after the prank I pulled on you? I'm surprised she left you to me now, if I'm being honest. Then again, it's easy to be brave as a kid who doesn't know the world yet. Now that she's had a taste of money and fame, I'm sure she won't risk that for some lowly detective who never could move on."

Darius balled his fist.

He could disarm Jon right then and there. Get the gun with or without one of them getting hit in the process and really give it to his personal ghost from the past.

But.

If the adult Jon was anything like the kid Jon, then there was an element of instability and callousness to him that could destroy any chances of Darius saving Winnie and her father.

Or Eve, if she decided to climb back through another window to try and save him.

Darius decided the best plan was to see what *Jon's* plan was—and quickly.

"If tying a kid up to a piece of industrial equipment to slowly get mutilated is a prank, then I'd hate to see what you think a good joke is."

Jon must not have liked the snark. He pushed the barrel of his gun harder into Darius's back. Normally, the pressure wouldn't bother him, but it just so happened to be the area that had been kicked repeatedly by the demon in humans' clothes behind him.

"Talking has always been *her* strong suit, not yours, Darius," Jon said. "You'd just get everyone killed with that mouth of yours. So I'd leave the snark to the professionals instead." He applied more pressure into the gun's barrel. "Speaking of professionals, I think it's time to leave before the colleagues I'm sure Evie has called in come running. I'd hate for you to lose the chance to save that lovely family I have all tied up, simply because the response time of Seven Roads's finest is actually impressive. Let's go."

Darius glanced at the nightstand.

Eve's phone was gone.

Relief pure and true moved through his chest.

He let Jon lead him outside to a black truck, its front partially damaged and a side mirror missing.

The relief that Eve had gotten away disappeared the second Jon cussed low.

"Looks like I underestimated Lana after all," he said. "I should have killed her first."

Darius caught his eye, his brow arching high.

Jon's mood switched gears again.

He laughed and looked back at the house.

"Hate to break it to you, Darius, but maybe little Evie didn't get away after all."

Chapter Twenty-One

Lana was fast. Even with an arm in a sling, an obvious head injury and a limp, she had her and Eve in a car and out to the steel mill's back entrance within what felt like the blink of an eye.

"This is where your friend shot us last time," Eve had to point out as they started walking to the residence halls. Caution tape could be seen across the porch of the men's building. Lana directed them toward the women's building on the other side.

"He wasn't supposed to shoot you," she said nonchalantly. "And he wasn't my friend."

Eve knew she shouldn't have followed Lana. She shouldn't have gotten into the car with her. She shouldn't have willingly come to a place no one would think to look for her. Yet, when Lana pushed open the front door and disappeared inside, Eve easily followed in step.

Like something had shifted between Eve and Darius, she could tell something had shifted behind the scenes for the criminals.

And whatever that was, it had pissed off Lana and created her own shift.

Though, Eve wasn't sure why the woman had come to her. She decided asking directly was the best way to deal with the woman who had wanted to kill her less than twenty-four hours ago.

"Why are you helping me? Helping Darius and Winnie and Price?"

Lana flipped on the lights. The inside of the women's residence hall wasn't as derelict as the men's had been. Still, Eve took care to keep closer to the wall and avoid the middle of the room until they were at a bunk bed with a mattress still intact. There was a laptop on its top, connected to a phone.

Lana sat heavily. Blood ran into her eye, and she cussed as she tried to wipe it out with her hand. The marker on her palm with her plea to Eve was a sharp contrast to the red.

"Because men are idiots," Lana ground out. "And instead of listening to the only smart one of them, they just keep calling in more men to be idiots." She blinked several times, her eye red from the irritation. Eve could now clearly see that her clothes were also torn and dirtied. She had definitely been through *something* since her stay at the hospital.

Eve had so many questions she wasn't sure which one to ask first. She decided to start with the odd choice of location.

"Why are we here, then? Why not just run if you're breaking your contract?"

Lana snorted.

"Scott Keys might be an idiot, but he's one with deep pockets and a right-hand who can control the rest of them just by snapping. I could disappear if I wanted, but there's someone I care about around here, and I don't want to spend the rest of my life running in the opposite direction."

Eve's adrenaline spiked for the second time that day.

"So Scott really *is* behind these attacks."

Lana nodded.

"Sanderson hired me, but it was heavily implied that Scott was funding my contract."

"That contract being…"

Lana reached down to a bag next to the bunk bed. For a moment, Eve felt foolish for trusting the woman. Now she was sure she was going to pay for being impulsive enough to follow the villain into the unknown.

However, all Lana pulled out was a small tin pack.

A first-aid symbol was on it.

She fumbled with the clasp, cussing lightly before responding.

"Technically, Scott wanted Mitchell dead, and you were just a piece of the story that made it all make sense. Woman tries to kill new husband for insurance money, but he kills her in self-defense before he succumbs to his injuries. Something that would be more believable after that family-lawyer guy was killed. Though, still not sure how he ended up at the wedding." Lana shook her head lightly. The first-aid kit finally opened. She pulled out a bundle of different-sized Band-Aids and set them on her lap. "But then that detective of yours kept showing up, and the rumors of you two having an affair started."

"Which is why you needed Mitchell to kill me and Darius," Eve realized.

Lana nodded.

"No matter who shot who first, the general public would have bought it," she said. "A jilted fiancé, a woman having an affair and a beloved local detective. Even if Mitchell or you survived somehow, the law around here would have come for your heads."

Lana continued to try and sort through the different-sized bandages.

"Scott already knew that Mitchell and I found evidence against him," Eve said. "That's why he pushed us to get married before we could get everything we needed. He needed it to look like I wanted the life insurance."

Lana surprised her. She didn't snort. She laughed.

"*This* is where I prove I'm a whole lot smarter than these men." Lana pointed to Eve, an unopened Band-Aid wrapper in her hand. "Scott never gave one thought to you, Miss Myers. He said Mitchell was the mastermind and that he only started dating you to gain access to Scott's day-to-day because of your job position. Scott and Sanderson? Not even for a second did they think you were important."

Eve instantly remembered what Lana had said the night before, after they had subdued her in the kitchen.

"But you realized last night that I wasn't just there," she offered.

Lana nodded.

"Mitchell killed a man to save you *and* Darius. Up until then I was under the impression that Mitchell was using *you*. Then I noticed that we had it backward. You were the one everyone kept looking at. You were in charge, even with the detective." She laughed again. "Men like Scott Keys rarely see women as anything other than pawns. Which is ironic, if you ask me."

The Band-Aid wrapper still wasn't open, and the blood along Lana's face kept dripping.

Eve sighed in frustration.

She grabbed the wrapper from the woman's hand and opened it.

"Does it really matter who found what, though?" she asked, taking the bandage out. "If Scott wants us all dead, then who cares who found the evidence? Evidence that I only have copies of, at that."

Lana's eyes widened as she pushed her hair out of the way. Eve placed the Band-Aid on the woman's skin.

She answered regardless of any surprise after the deed was done.

"It matters because they've been underestimating you," Lana said. "You're just some little pawn they want to move around to make the story of two guys fighting good."

Eve didn't like that. She patted the Band-Aid lightly to make sure it stuck. When she stepped back Lana was staring up at her with a new ferocity.

"To be underestimated is to be overlooked, and *that's* why they won't see you coming until it's too late."

"You want to—what?—ambush Scott? I won't help you kill anyone," Eve cautioned. "Even if it's him."

Lana waved the thought off.

"Scott, as far as I can tell, is untouchable for the simple fact that I'm not sure who all he's hired around here—around him," she defended. "As far as I can tell right now, you, the detective, Mitchell and that kid I beat up last night are the only ones who seem to want Scott and the rest of us behind bars. But since this new guy just appeared on the board, the only piece I could grab without getting myself tangled up was you. Everyone else is either missing or with him."

"You mean Winnie and Price Collins."

Lana nodded.

"Before this scar guy tried to kill me, he fished for some info, and I fished right on back," she said. "He took the girl, and the dad followed, and now they're somewhere in town as leverage for the detective. The detective is supposed to be leverage for you, and then *you* are supposed to be the leverage for Mitchell. Who, by the way, has really gone to ground. I don't even think Scott knows where his brother is."

Relief went through Eve at that. At least she knew Mitchell was most likely safe with Deputy Gavin. She hoped he could stay that way until everything was said and done.

Said and done with everyone she loved safe.

"But you knew I was with Darius," Eve said instead. "And this new guy didn't."

Lana laughed again.

"I noticed a pattern with the two of you," she said. "Wherever one of you is, the other is too. Something else these guys hadn't picked up on."

The relief Eve felt because of Mitchell turned to a clamp around her heart.

"We could call the sheriff," Eve tried. "Darius trusts him, and I trust Darius."

Lana didn't say no, but her skepticism was loud.

"What if Scott has someone in the sheriff's department? Or, what if there are more people like me out there, following law enforcement and reporting back?" She shook her head. "I don't know where your detective is, but I can guarantee that if Scott thinks his plan isn't working, he'll let that new boy of his kill Detective Williams quick."

Eve didn't like that.

Not one bit.

Still, she didn't understand what Lana was thinking.

"What are we supposed to do, then?" Eve asked. "Find Darius and then—what?—storm in, guns blazing? You might be good with a gun, but I've only ever shot at you."

Lana finally motioned to the laptop open next to her.

"The guy who got me out of the deputy's cruiser had this in his truck. Before I realized he was going to try and off me, I grabbed it and came here. When I saw the files pulled up on the screen, that's when I realized this must have been what had Scott and Sanderson all up in arms." She handed the laptop over to Eve. "So you tell me. How do we use five flight-plan records to push a king like Scott Keys off his throne?"

"Flight plans? There are copies on here?"

Eve was so curious she sat down next to the woman who had been her biggest enemy the night before.

"They look like they came straight from some private airfield's cataloging system, but past that I don't know what it is that's so special about them."

Lana was right.

Eve took a moment to look through the first one.

"This is actual physical evidence that has Toby flying out to areas near the towns I think Scott destroyed before saving them… It's not just someone on the phone or a blurry security picture that puts him en route."

"And this could help incriminate someone as power-ful as Scott?"

Eve shook her head to the obvious surprise of Lana.

"Not just this, but we believe *this* is the start of the in-vestigation that would uncover the truth. And seeing as how everything happened after we realized there *were* flight plans, I'm assuming we're right about it."

Lana said she didn't need any more information. Instead, she started rattling off ways they could use the information to make a deal or trap or frame Scott or *something.* Eve's at-tention had strayed to a detail she hadn't processed before.

"Five flight records," she said, interrupting Lana.

"What?"

Eve touched the laptop's screen with one hand and used the other on the trackpad to scroll through the pages.

"There are five here, but we were only ever able to find

four records." She stopped at one file. "We nixed this one because when Toby landed, he used a rental car that took him in the opposite direction for a golf tournament."

Lana leaned in a little to look at the file in question.

"And why do we care about Toby?" she asked.

Eve opened her mouth to point out that, as Scott's right-hand man, he was someone that needed to be cared about.

But she stopped herself short.

"You never said *right-hand man*," Eve said instead. "You just said *right-hand*." She felt her eyes widen as it finally dawned on her. "And you never said *Toby*. You just said *Sanderson*."

Eve scanned the document she had once dismissed.

The same name was on all five.

Apparently, she had also overlooked someone.

Toby Sanderson was dead.

His wife, Maria, stepped over his body wearing heels.

Darius watched as she made her way over to him, smile rimmed with dark red lipstick.

"Honestly, I can spin this just as easy as the soap-opera storyline Scott has been trying to play out since we got to this horrible little town," she said. "Except, I'm not going to waste my time waiting for all of you to do your parts."

Maria didn't have a gun in her hand, but she did have a Jon.

He was leaning against one of the four large steel beams that had been holding up the warehouse since the last time he and Darius had been there.

Now instead of a rotary tiller, he was cuffed to a metal pole sticking out of the concrete. Whatever it used to be attached to had long since been sawn away.

"It was you who engineered the attacks on those towns—

on Seven Roads—through the years," Darius said. "Not Toby."

That had become glaringly clear the second Jon had walked him inside and around the socialite's dead body. They had gotten the wrong Sanderson, and now the right one seemed to be tickled by the mess-up.

"To be honest, it's kind of nice to get the credit for once."

Maria paused next to a crate covered in dust. With her heel she hooked the handle and managed to flip it onto its side. She was elegant in the action of sitting down on it, but Darius could still see her husband's blood on the bottom of her shoes.

She caught his gaze and gave her shoe a once-over before smiling again.

"See, I've always had a knack for breaking things," she said. "Rules, boundaries, people. And wouldn't you know it, towns too."

Darius recalled Eve's notes on the first town she had suspected that Scott had purposefully crippled.

"The corruption case in Culver," he remembered.

Maria snapped her fingers, smile only widening.

"Who knew a few whispers here and there could detonate the entire infrastructure of that little no-nothing town," she said, clearly delighted. "Truthfully, I didn't even mean for it to happen. It was like playing dolls."

"Your version of dolls destroyed hundreds of innocent lives, one way or the other," Darius pointed out.

Maria waved her hand through the air, as if shooing an annoying fly that was buzzing around her.

"But then who came in and made it all better with all his money and all his charm? Scott the White Knight Keys. A hero that I had summoned for a problem that I had created."

"And let me guess. Scott thought it was his idea."

Maria nodded, her hair not moving an inch from its hair-spray hold.

"That's the beauty of all of this, isn't it?" she said. "I get the power, the money and the high without the responsibility if things go south. Because who's going to look at the charming hero and the spoiled wife of his friend and think *I'm* even involved?"

Maria looked over her shoulder at her husband's body. She sighed.

"Even he had no clue what he was looking at, after your girlfriend talked about those records."

For the first time since Darius had been cuffed and Maria had entered the warehouse, the woman's mirth seemed to ebb.

The dark red of her frown made the apparent wealth she was wrapped in seem more sinister than before.

"Eve, Eve, Eve," she said. "Unlike Scott, I don't need to kill her, you *and* Mitchell all together. I can do two birds and one stone now." Maria snapped her fingers again. Jon pushed himself off the beam to stand tall. "You said she would come for him?"

Jon nodded.

"Guaranteed."

Maria swung her gaze back to Darius.

"Also unlike Scott, I don't ignore new information." Her fingernails were painted red. Darius could see them clearly as she pointed his way. "Like when Jon here reached out to our White Knight saying he could help? I didn't discount it. No, I listened to what he had to say. And, Detective, do you know what he had to say?"

Darius kept his mouth shut.

He had already profiled the woman across from him. She was a yapper.

And yappers didn't really need feedback to keep yapping. Maria proved him right.

"He told me that the fastest way to get Evelyn Myers is to get you." A smile twisted up the corners of her lips. She continued, sounding as wicked as she looked. "And then? All I have to do is make you scream."

Chapter Twenty-Two

Everyone's problems boiled down to one issue and one issue only.

Everyone had underestimated a woman.

Lana had realized her mistake first. So she had saved Eve from Jon's clutches, gambling that the save would also buy Darius more time.

Eve had realized her mistake second.

Maria had been the person at Scott's side the entire time. The spoiled rich socialite in designer clothes, always looking bored and annoyed and superior. Never in touch with anyone below her status. Always a passive-aggressive word or ten to people like Eve.

A woman to avoided for sanity's sake.

Scott had probably never seen her coming.

Lana had, and that's why she had jumped ship once Jon Decanter, ghost from the past, had joined Maria's forces. Lana knew Maria would be the one to clean house for Scott, and not even she thought she could outrun her forever.

Eve knew Maria had already realized her mistake since she had gone with Jon to the warehouse. If they had wanted to lure Mitchell out, they would have used another location. But Maria wanted Eve, and Jon gave her the quickest path there.

As Eve walked through the unlocked door, she saw the satisfaction pass over Maria's expression. She stood from her seat on an old box and waved. Darius, behind her, was alive and cuffed to something.

If Eve hadn't been boiling with rage at the man between them, she would have cried in relief.

"Oh, Evelyn, how sweet," Maria started. "You really do seem to love the detective. Oh dear, I guess Mitchell was indeed just a match of convenience. Scott is going to be so upset when he finds out he was played like this. Especially when he thought his brother was the one playing you."

She giggled.

Eve ignored her.

She had taken a few steps inside the warehouse, the door closing behind her. She had no weapon. No way to defend herself. No foolproof or safe plan to free Darius and escape unharmed. No way to trap, disarm or make the secret mastermind behind the investigation that had consumed Eve's life over the last year willingly give themselves up.

Which might have been for the better.

Because the second she saw Jon, she was suddenly the same little girl she had been when she had seen him last.

Eve locked eyes with Jon.

The only human she had ever hated.

When her voice came out, not even Eve recognized it.

"What was the last thing I told you, Jon?" she growled out.

Darius said her name.

Eve took a step forward.

"Don't tell me you've already forgotten," she added. "Not after I made sure to make it memorable."

Jon's nostrils flared. She could see that clearly even from the hundred or so feet she stood away from him. Just like the scar at the side of his face.

It was small, smaller than the one on her hand. Much smaller than the one on Darius's back.

"You've got some nerve," he bit out.

Eve rolled up her left jacket sleeve. She did the other one next.

"*You're* the one with the nerve, Jon. Not even Fate would have been stupid enough to put us back together. That had to be you." Eve shared a quick look with Maria. Her mouth hung open in a confused smile. "Let me guess. He saw something about me or Darius in the news and begged to be a part of your unnecessarily complicated scheme to frame and kill us. And you decided, *why not?*"

Maria's smile faded, but her words still held confidence as she responded.

"So Jon *was* telling the truth," she said. "He has a special relationship with the two of you. How interesting." Maria took a few steps back so she could see both of them more easily. Her shifting gave Eve a clear view of a body on the floor near the opposite wall.

Toby.

His shoes weren't Italian leather, but she recognized them all the same.

Eve didn't have time to linger on him.

Just as she didn't have time to look at Darius.

Instead, she doubled down on a plan that might get her killed.

"If you really want to hear something fun, ask him how he got that scar," Eve poked. She tapped the side of her face. The same spot Jon was touching with the hand not holding a gun.

A gun that Eve was sure he was about to be itching to use.

Maria, ever a gossip, was already locked in.

"How *did* you get that scar, Mr. Decanter?" she asked. "Do tell."

Jon had always looked like a little worm of a human. As a child, he had never had a redeeming quality to him in Eve's young eyes. Nothing had changed. His face pinched, his shoulders tightened with rage, she knew that despite every effort he was most likely employing, the memory of their last meeting was replaying in detail in his head.

He didn't want to answer Maria, that much was obvious.

But Maria wasn't a woman used to being disappointed.

Her voice lowered into a command that might have alarmed Eve had it been under different circumstances.

"How did you get that scar?"

Jon's hand twitched. A smile clawed its way upward from his frown. It was as fake as a sociopath could make it.

His words came out bitter, regardless of the form of his mouth.

"Eve gave it to me when we were kids. She said it was a warning, and that, if I ever so much as showed my face in front of Darius again, she'd make sure it was a face no one would recognize after that."

Maria whirled around, full focus on Eve. The surprise affected her entire body. She was nearly dancing in delight.

"Eve!" she exclaimed. "Look at you! How vicious! Maybe I should have hired you instead of this one. Who knew you had it in you!"

It was true, and it wasn't completely true.

Eve had, in fact, tracked the kid Jon down and threatened him. But the scar on his face had been an accident. After doctoring Darius's back and her hand, they had decided to not tell anyone about the incident. It hadn't been for Jon's benefit, but for fear that the incident would get their parents to reevaluate their living situations. That, because they had been left alone so much, something would need to change. Darius had a godmother out of state; Eve could have gone to a summer program at the school. Or, if their parents hadn't decided to shuffle them off somewhere to be safe, there was always the possibility that the two of them spending so much time together would have been frowned on.

So little Eve and Darius had kept the assault and its brutality to themselves.

But that hadn't meant Eve had let Jon off the hook.

She had gotten him out of his house that night and made it sound like she would tell the adults if he ever tried to get near them again.

That had got Jon mad.

He had lunged at her. It was only good luck on her part that his grandmother's backyard was uneven and covered in dirt. He had slipped and fallen. Eve, knowing this was the only advantage she would get, had jumped on him.

Only a few minutes later, with blood covering her hands, did she realize that a rock had embedded in his cheek. Instead of pointing this out to him, instead of panicking, instead of going for help, Darius's scream of pain had echoed in her mind, and she decided to get herself one more advantage.

She had pushed the rock into his skin.

Not a lot but enough to make *him* scream.

Then, she had threatened him with those vicious words.

As an adult, Eve knew that she had been wrong to do it. That there were better ways to avenge violence.

But there was nothing she could do to change it.

So she did as she had done and leaned into the idea that she had caused the scar on purpose.

"Yet here you are," she said now. "Despite my very clear warning."

Jon let out a sound that was between a growl and a yell. He sounded possessed. Maria seemed to enjoy it all the more. She actually clapped.

"Wow, you just have to love small towns," she said. "They really are like soap operas. Everyone has some kind of tawdry back story. Surely there's something you want to add before we end this episode, Detective Williams?"

She started to turn back around, but Eve was faster.

"Maria," she called out, quickly, "do you want to know one more secret first?"

Maria paused but nodded, still clearly enjoying herself like they were at some kind of party or weird double date.

"Of course! Get it all off your chest now."

This time, Eve mirrored her smile. Her voice rang clear throughout the old warehouse.

"The tractor-supply business who owned this place? They might have gone out of business, but you want to know what they *didn't* do?" Eve's leg muscles tensed in anticipation. Her heartbeat started to gallop.

Maria was completely unaware of the change about to rock her world.

She simply raised an eyebrow in question.

Eve was happy to give her the answer.

"After all of these years, they never repaired that window."

Jon understood first. He whirled around, gun raised, but it was too late.

Eve ran for cover behind the collection of dust-covered crates closest to her just as two shots rang out.

Maria yelled.

Jon made a noise.

Then silence.

Eve scrambled to her feet again, already yelling Darius's name.

MARIA HAD BEEN RIGHT. Living in a small town sure felt like watching a soap opera sometimes.

Darius, handcuffed to a random metal pipe in an old, abandoned warehouse, kept in check by the source of his childhood trauma, while the love of his life was in danger?

Well, it all felt very dramatic.

And maybe if the main villain had been even a little bit less dramatic and her lackey less emotional, Maria would have noticed that Eve wasn't just talking to talk. She wasn't trying to twist the metaphorical knife into the old wound of Jon Decanter just to remind him of the scarring defeat he had suffered by the hand of the little protective girl down the street.

Not that Darius had understood that himself at first, though. It wasn't until he realized Eve was purposefully not looking at him that he started paying attention to what was happening outside their past's retelling.

Someone had climbed through the window that Eve had broken during her rescue when they were kids. And it wasn't until he felt that person fiddling with the lock on his handcuff that he understood that Eve hadn't just run in as a sacrifice to try and save him.

Instead of making herself bait like she had done the day before in the meeting room in front of Scott and Toby, Evelyn Myers had made herself different once she had walked into that warehouse.

She had made herself a distraction.

And by God, it had worked.

Darius had run through Jon like a sledgehammer through a thin piece of paper.

Jon managed two shots, but they were just the last cries of a dying man.

Darius heard the crack of Jon's head hitting the cement floor before he felt it.

He knew Jon was gone as he secured the gun and turned it on Maria. Still, his body couldn't help but stay alert while standing.

"Move and I shoot," Darius yelled at the woman. The warning came out at the same time Eve yelled for him.

She didn't wait for him to answer her.

Not that Darius expected that she would wait.

The sound of her shoes slapping against the floor echoed around them as she ran past Maria and right to him.

Darius was about to warn her to get behind him when the person who had freed him spoke up instead.

"Dang, Eve, let's make sure our villainess doesn't have a weapon first before you go all gooey on our hero."

Darius tensed as he recognized the voice.

The woman known as Lana stepped slowly into view next to them. Her arm was still in a sling from where he had broken her wrist. She had a Band-Aid on her forehead.

The most surprising detail?

Eve rolled her eyes at the woman.

"Listen, I'm the one who is usually sneaking in through windows," Eve said. "Being out in the open like this is new for me."

In another surprising turn of events, Lana actually sighed.

"I don't know if anyone has told you this yet, but there are these things called doors, Miss Myers. And I'm sure no one, not even Detective Williams here, would blame you if you started using them."

Maybe it was the adrenaline wearing off, maybe it was shock at everything that had happened since he had woken up that morning or maybe it was because of the sheer amount of relief flooding his system at knowing that the woman he loved was okay that he did something out of character for the situation.

Despite himself, Darius laughed.

Chapter Twenty-Three

Scott Keys went down in a blaze of glory.

A blaze of glory that was documented so well that the news stories went viral across the country.

He had tried to make his brother look like a victim of a greedy new wife and her lover, and instead he had ended up playing the main role of the greedy millionaire versus the underdogs.

At least Maria Sanderson had been quick to take her name out of the credits.

Once the feds had gotten involved and officially opened an investigation into the Keys Foundation and the man at its helm, she had made a deal. She had sold Scott out completely before ever seeing the inside of a jail cell.

She might have skipped prison altogether had another woman not stepped forward and made her own deal.

Lana had, as far as anyone could tell—and by her own insistence—never actually killed anyone. Not in Seven Roads and not during any of her previous contracts. Darius wasn't sure he believed her, but when she provided audio recordings and physical evidence of being hired and instructed by Maria to kidnap and kill Eve, Darius and Mitchell, he couldn't help but feel a bit grateful to her. Especially when Eve explained that Lana had been the one to get her out of the house when Jon had shown up.

"If she hadn't shown up at the window, I would have walked into the living room with the two of you like it was nothing," Eve had said, during their ride in the ambulance after the rest of the sheriff's department had come to the warehouse. "Without her, all of us might have met a much different outcome. Even if she did do it for herself."

Darius didn't push his opinion on the matter, but he did decide to thank Lana before she was taken away in cuffs.

"You could have run," Darius had told her. "Thank you for staying with Eve instead."

Lana had surprised him with a laugh.

"To be honest, if she had been my boss, I think I would have done whatever she asked of me. Evelyn is pure loyalty. Even us bad guys can appreciate that." Lana had paused before following the federal agent to their car. "I know my words don't mean much, but just in case no one has told you yet, I think you might want to marry that woman."

And Darius did.

Three months later, in between their childhood homes and the windows that had shaped their entire lives, Darius and Eve were married.

Darius wore a nice suit, Eve had a dress that poofed out at the bottom, and they even managed to find folding white chairs like Mrs. Dunphy used to have when they were kids. Which, according to Eve, had been an important detail. Her father walked her down the aisle while Theo and Winnie stood on either side of an arch her father had made by hand.

After Winnie and Price had been ambushed by Jon and the one last hired hand Maria had running around Seven Roads before being arrested, Theo and Price's wife JJ had raised hell to find and rescue them. Unlike Jon, their attacker had survived their retribution and had gone to prison, where no deals were made and no promises of an early release were given.

Since then Darius's Oil and Water duo had become somewhat inseparable.

So it only made sense when they became the new tenants of the house next door. At first Eve would pass by Darius's old bedroom window and wave at across to Winnie, who had taken over Eve's former bedroom.

Then, one day, Winnie moved out.

And right into the main bedroom with Theo.

The whole of Seven Roads was more excited for their wedding years later than they had ever been about Mitchell Keys and Evelyn Myers tying the knot. It almost felt like a holiday as nearly all the town showed up in their finest and watched as the oldest children of the sheriff's department said *I do*. Their wedding reception became a reunion all its own for the department.

The men and women who had spent their careers protecting Seven Roads to the best of their abilities gathered around for a toast about the past.

"I came to Seven Roads because I wanted quiet," Liam started. The sheriff looked at his wife, Blake, and grinned. "Now I live in the loudest house in the zip code." Everyone laughed, but no one disagreed. They had six kids, a live-in mother and father-in-law, and two dogs. *Loud* didn't cover it.

Price went next, raising his glass as his wife JJ currently held one of their surprise set of twins. Winnie had the other on her hip as she swayed back and forth with Theo on the dance floor.

"I wanted to leave the second Winnie was old enough

to move out," Price said. "Now we're looking at building a house down the road."

Rose went next, her husband towering over her, a little girl fast asleep against his chest. She was the first of four who they had adopted from foster care, taking their family from three to six. Something that her husband James boasted about quite often.

"I always knew this Seven Roads was where I belonged, but I'm glad you boys finally figured it out for yourselves," Rose said, sassy as ever. "Though, I did snag the best mechanic in town, so I guess there's something I changed for us."

They all did a quick cheers for that, laughter mixed in.

Deputy Gavin went next, already grinning ear to ear.

"I went from thinking love was dead to marrying a millionaire, so I can't complain."

That got Darius really good. He and Eve couldn't hold back as they looked at the millionaire in question, currently talking the ear off JJ's brother at the bar.

Mitchell Keys hadn't only taken over the Keys Foundation once Scott had gone to prison. He and Eve had transformed it into something entirely different and absolutely impactful. Making the headquarters in Seven Roads had not only helped the town with new jobs, it had also given Mitchell and his deputy time to fall in love. A love that the department had been happy to endorse in place of his brother.

It also had made Eve jump for joy.

One night, in between the sheets, Eve had admitted to Darius that at one point, she had been afraid that she really had missed out on life.

"But now I have a best friend who I see every day, a job I really care about that makes a difference *and* I got to keep a promise I made a long time ago." She had sighed in contentedness. "I guess I didn't miss out on life. I was just waiting for you to start it."

Darius had seconded that sentiment.

Now he raised his glass, the last of them to speak, and said what he had always known to be true.

"I accepted a life in Seven Roads that only saw me growing old and grumpy by myself," Darius said. He looked to Eve. He could hear their children's squeals of laughter from the dance floor. He smiled. "Turns out I was just waiting for the drama to come back to town."

Eve was the loudest as the group around him burst into laughter at that before they all lifted their glasses together.

"It's been a wild ride these past few years with all of you," the sheriff called out. "And I wouldn't have wanted it any other way. So here's to McCoy County's finest. May we go to the dance floor now to embarrass the younger generation with dance moves that will embarrass us in the morning!"

The group all yelled and cheered and clinked their glasses together before following their sheriff to do just that.

Darius, however, caught Eve's hand before she could make it too far.

She giggled as he pulled her into his arms.

He cut that giggle off with a kiss born from a love that had never once wavered, no matter how many years had gone by.

Eve returned it with an answering love.

Then she swatted him away with laughter in her eyes.

"You better not try and get out of dancing with me, Detective Williams." She pointed at him, a beautiful smile playing at her lips. "You have to listen to me no matter what, remember? Your life is mine, after all."

It was a joke that they often exchanged through the years. The promise that Eve had made to his mother that Darius's life would forever be hers. And while no one who heard the story thought the promise made by a child had been taken seriously, he knew better.

Darius had always been Eve's.

And as he followed his wife to the dance floor surrounded by their loved ones, Darius knew without a doubt that he always would be.

* * * * *

Get up to 4 Free Books!

We'll send you 2 free books from each series you try PLUS a free Mystery Gift.

FREE Value Over $25

Both the **Harlequin Intrigue®** and **Harlequin® Romantic Suspense** series feature compelling novels filled with heart-racing action-packed romance that will keep you on the edge of your seat.

YES! Please send me 2 FREE novels from the Harlequin Intrigue or Harlequin Romantic Suspense series and my FREE gift (gift is worth about $10 retail). After receiving them, if I don't wish to receive any more books, I can return the shipping statement marked "cancel." If I don't cancel, I will receive 6 brand-new Harlequin Intrigue Larger-Print books every month and be billed just $7.19 each in the U.S. or $7.99 each in Canada, or 4 brand-new Harlequin Romantic Suspense books every month and be billed just $6.39 each in the U.S. or $7.19 each in Canada, a savings of 20% off the cover price. It's quite a bargain! Shipping and handling is just 50¢ per book in the U.S. and $1.25 per book in Canada.* I understand that accepting the 2 free books and gift places me under no obligation to buy anything. I can always return a shipment and cancel at any time by calling the number below. The free books and gift are mine to keep no matter what I decide.

Choose one: ☐ **Harlequin Intrigue Larger-Print** (199/399 BPA G36Y) ☐ **Harlequin Romantic Suspense** (240/340 BPA G36Y) ☐ **Or Try Both!** (199/399 & 240/340 BPA G36Z)

Name (please print)

Address   Apt. #

City   State/Province   Zip/Postal Code

Email: Please check this box ☐ if you would like to receive newsletters and promotional emails from Harlequin Enterprises ULC and its affiliates. You can unsubscribe anytime.

Mail to the Harlequin Reader Service:
IN U.S.A.: P.O. Box 1341, Buffalo, NY 14240-8531
IN CANADA: P.O. Box 603, Fort Erie, Ontario L2A 5X3

Want to explore our other series or interested in ebooks? Visit www.ReaderService.com or call 1-800-873-8635.

*Terms and prices subject to change without notice. Prices do not include sales taxes, which will be charged (if applicable) based on your state or country of residence. Canadian residents will be charged applicable taxes. Offer not valid in Quebec. This offer is limited to one order per household. Books received may not be as shown. Not valid for current subscribers to the Harlequin Intrigue or Harlequin Romantic Suspense series. All orders subject to approval. Credit or debit balances in a customer's account(s) may be offset by any other outstanding balance owed by or to the customer. Please allow 4 to 6 weeks for delivery. Offer available while quantities last.

Your Privacy—Your information is being collected by Harlequin Enterprises ULC, operating as Harlequin Reader Service. For a complete summary of the information we collect, how we use this information and to whom it is disclosed, please visit our privacy notice located at https://corporate.harlequin.com/privacy-notice. Notice to California Residents – Under California law, you have specific rights to control and access your data. For more information on these rights and how to exercise them, visit https://corporate.harlequin.com/california-privacy. For additional information for residents of other U.S. states that provide their residents with certain rights with respect to personal data, visit https://corporate.harlequin.com/other-state-residents-privacy-rights/.

HIHRS25